Henry James

Henry James OM (15 April 1843 – 28 February 1916) was an American-British author regarded as a key transitional figure between literary realism and literary modernism, and is considered by many to be among the greatest novelists in the English language. He was the son of Henry James Sr. and the brother of renowned philosopher and psychologist William James and diarist Alice James.

He is best known for a number of novels dealing with the social and marital interplay between émigré Americans, English people, and continental Europeans. Examples of such novels include The Portrait of a Lady, The Ambassadors, and The Wings of the Dove. His later works were increasingly experimental. In describing the internal states of mind and social dynamics of his characters, James often made use of a style in which ambiguous or contradictory motives and impressions were overlaid or juxtaposed in the discussion of a character's psyche.(Source: Wikipedia)

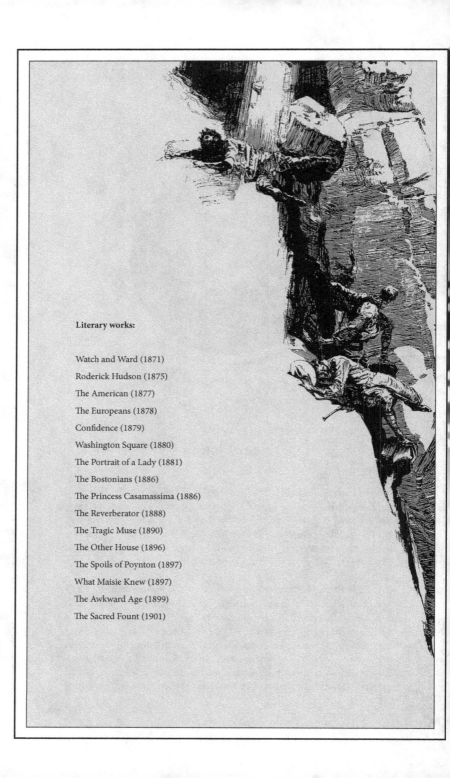

Literary works:

Watch and Ward (1871)
Roderick Hudson (1875)
The American (1877)
The Europeans (1878)
Confidence (1879)
Washington Square (1880)
The Portrait of a Lady (1881)
The Bostonians (1886)
The Princess Casamassima (1886)
The Reverberator (1888)
The Tragic Muse (1890)
The Other House (1896)
The Spoils of Poynton (1897)
What Maisie Knew (1897)
The Awkward Age (1899)
The Sacred Fount (1901)

THE
WORKS
OF
HENRY JAMES
VOL. 07 (OF 36)

GEORGINA'S REASONS

GLASSES

An Imprint of Moon Classics LLC

A Wholly Owned Subsidiary of Queenior LLC

A Melodragon Company

Copyright © 2020

First Printing: 2020

ISBN 978-1-6627-1560-0 (Paperback)

ISBN 978-1-6627-1561-7 (Hardcover)

Published by Moon Classics

www.moonclassics.com

Contents

THE
WORKS
OF
HENRY JAMES
VOL. 07 (OF 36)

GEORGINA'S REASONS

PART I.

I.

She was certainly a singular girl, and if he felt at the end that he did n't know her nor understand her, it is not surprising that he should have felt it at the beginning. But he felt at the beginning what he did not feel at the end, that her singularity took the form of a charm which—once circumstances had made them so intimate—it was impossible to resist or conjure away. He had a strange impression (it amounted at times to a positive distress, and shot through the sense of pleasure—morally speaking—with the acuteness of a sudden twinge of neuralgia) that it would be better for each of them that they should break off short and never see each other again. In later years he called this feeling a foreboding, and remembered two or three occasions when he had been on the point of expressing it to Georgina. Of course, in fact, he never expressed it; there were plenty of good reasons for that. Happy love is not disposed to assume disagreeable duties, and Raymond Benyon's love was happy, in spite of grave presentiments, in spite of the singularity of his mistress and the insufferable rudeness of her parents. She was a tall, fair girl, with a beautiful cold eye and a smile of which the perfect sweetness, proceeding from the lips, was full of compensation; she had auburn hair of a hue that could be qualified as nothing less than gorgeous, and she seemed to move through life with a stately grace, as she would have walked through an old-fashioned minuet. Gentlemen connected with the navy have the advantage of seeing many types of women; they are able to compare the ladies of New York with those of Valparaiso, and those of Halifax with those of the Cape of Good Hope. Eaymond Benyon had had these advantages, and being very fond of women he had learnt his lesson; he was in a position to appreciate Georgina Gressie's fine points. She looked like a duchess,—I don't mean that in foreign ports Benyon had associated with duchesses,—and she took everything so seriously. That was flattering for the young man, who was only a lieutenant, detailed for duty at the Brooklyn navy-yard, without a penny in the world but his pay, with a set of plain, numerous, seafaring, God-fearing relations in New Hampshire, a considerable appearance of talent, a feverish, disguised ambition, and a slight impediment in his speech.

He was a spare, tough young man, his dark hair was straight and fine, and his face, a trifle pale, was smooth and carefully drawn. He stammered a little, blushing when he did so, at long intervals. I scarcely know how he appeared on shipboard, but on shore, in his civilian's garb, which was of the neatest, he had as little as possible an aroma of winds and waves. He was neither salt nor brown, nor red, nor particularly "hearty." He never twitched up his trousers, nor, so far as one could see, did he, with his modest, attentive manner, carry himself as one accustomed to command. Of course, as a subaltern, he had more to do in the way of obeying. He looked as if he followed some sedentary calling, and was, indeed, supposed to be decidedly intellectual. He was a lamb with women, to whose charms he was, as I have hinted, susceptible; but with men he was different, and, I believe, as much of a wolf as was necessary. He had a manner of adoring the handsome, insolent queen of his affections (I will explain in a moment why I call her insolent); indeed, he looked up to her literally as well as sentimentally; for she was the least bit the taller of the two. He had met her the summer before, on the piazza of a hotel at Fort Hamilton, to which, with a brother officer, in a dusty buggy, he had driven over from Brooklyn to spend a tremendously hot Sunday,—the kind of day when the navy-yard was loathsome; and the acquaintance had been renewed by his calling in Twelfth Street on New-Year's Day,—a considerable time to wait for a pretext, but which proved the impression had not been transitory. The acquaintance ripened, thanks to a zealous cultivation (on his part) of occasions which Providence, it must be confessed, placed at his disposal none too liberally; so that now Georgina took up all his thoughts and a considerable part of his time. He was in love with her, beyond a doubt; but he could not flatter himself that she was in love with him, though she appeared willing (what was so strange) to quarrel with her family about him. He did n't see how she could really care for him,—she seemed marked out by nature for so much greater a fortune; and he used to say to her, "Ah, you don't—there's no use talking, you don't—really care for me at all!" To which she answered, "Really? You are very particular. It seems to me it's real enough if I let you touch one of my fingertips! "That was one of her ways of being insolent Another was simply her manner of looking at him, or at other people (when they spoke to her), with her hard, divine blue eye,—looking quietly, amusedly, with the air of considering (wholly from her own point of view) what they might have said, and then turning her head or her back, while, without taking the trouble to answer them, she broke into a short, liquid, irrelevant laugh. This may seem to contradict what I said just now about her taking the young lieutenant in the navy seriously. What I mean is that she appeared to take him more seriously than she took anything else. She said to him once, "At any rate you have the merit of not being a shop-keeper;" and it was by this epithet she was pleased to designate most of the young men who at that time flourished in the best society of New York. Even if she had rather a free way of expressing general indifference, a young lady is supposed to be serious enough when she consents to marry you. For the rest, as regards a certain haughtiness that might be observed in Geoigina Gressie, my story will probably throw sufficient light upon it She remarked to Benyon once that it was none of his business why she liked him, but that, to please herself, she did n't mind telling him she thought the great Napoleon, before he was celebrated, before he had command of the army of Italy, must have looked something like him; and she sketched in a few words the sort of figure she imagined the incipient Bonaparte to have been,—short, lean, pale, poor, intellectual, and with a tremendous future under his hat Benyon asked himself whether *he* had a tremendous future, and what in the world Geoigina expected of him in the coming years. He was flattered at the comparison, he was ambitious enough not to be frightened at it, and he guessed that she perceived a certain analogy between herself and the Empress Josephine. She would make a very good empress. That was true; Georgina was remarkably imperial. This may not at first seem to make it more clear why she should take into her favor an aspirant who, on the face of the matter, was not original, and whose Corsica was a flat New England seaport; but it afterward became plain that he owed his brief happiness—it was very brief—to her father's opposition; her father's and her mother's, and even her uncles' and her aunts'. In those days, in New York, the different members of a family took an interest in its alliances, and the house of Gressie looked askance at an engagement between the most beautiful of its daughters and a young man who was not in a paying business. Georgina declared that they were meddlesome and vulgar,—she could sacrifice her own people, in that way, without a scruple,—and Benyon's position improved from the moment that Mr. Gressie—ill-advised Mr. Gressie—ordered the girl to have nothing to do with him. Georgina was imperial in this—that she wouldn't put up with an order. When, in the house in Twelfth Street, it began to be talked about that she had better be sent to Europe with some eligible friend, Mrs. Portico, for instance, who was always planning to go, and who wanted as a companion some young mind, fresh from manuals and extracts, to serve as a fountain of history and geography,—when this scheme for getting Georgina out of the way began to be aired, she immediately said to Raymond Benyon, "Oh, yes, I 'll marry you!" She said it in such an off-hand way that, deeply as he desired her, he was almost tempted to answer, "But, my dear, have you really thought about it?"

This little drama went on, in New York, in the ancient days, when Twelfth Street had but lately ceased to be suburban, when the squares had wooden palings, which were not often painted; when there were poplars in important thoroughfares and pigs in the lateral ways; when the theatres were miles distant from Madison Square, and the battered rotunda of Castle Garden echoed with expensive vocal music; when "the park" meant the grass-plats of the city hall, and the Bloomingdale road was an eligible drive; when Hoboken, of a summer afternoon, was a genteel resort, and the handsomest house in town was on the corner of the Fifth Avenue and Fifteenth Street. This will strike the modern reader, I fear, as rather a primitive epoch; but I am not sure that the strength of human passions is in proportion to the elongation of a city. Several of them, at any rate, the most robust and most familiar,—love, ambition, jealousy, resentment, greed,—subsisted in considerable force in the little circle at which we have glanced, where a view by no means favorable was taken of Raymond Benyon's attentions to Miss Gressie. Unanimity was a family trait among these people (Georgina was an exception), especially in regard to the important concerns of life, such as marriages and closing scenes. The Gressies hung together; they were accustomed to do well for themselves and for each other. They did everything well: got themselves born well (they thought it excellent to be born a Gressie), lived well, married well, died well, and managed to be well spoken of afterward. In deference to this last-mentioned habit, I must be careful what I say of them. They took an interest in each other's concerns, an interest that could never be regarded as of a meddlesome nature, inasmuch as they all thought alike about all their affairs, and interference took the happy form of congratulation and encouragement. These affairs were invariably lucky, and, as a general thing, no Gressie had anything to do but feel that another Gressie had been almost as shrewd and decided as he himself would have been. The great exception to that, as I have said, was this case of Georgina, who struck such a false note, a note that startled them all, when she told her father that she should like to unite herself to a young man engaged in the least paying business that any Gressie had ever heard of. Her two sisters had married into the most flourishing firms, and it was not to be thought of that—with twenty cousins growing up around her—she should put down the standard of success. Her mother had told her a fortnight before this that she must request Mr. Benyon to cease coming to the house; for hitherto his suit had been of the most public and resolute character. He had been conveyed up town from the Brooklyn ferry, in the "stage," on certain evenings, had asked for Miss Georgina at the door of the house in Twelfth Street, and had sat with her in the front parlor if her parents happened to occupy the back, or in the back if the family had disposed itself in the front. Georgina, in her way, was a dutiful girl, and she immediately repeated her mother's admonition to Beuyon. He was not surprised, for though he was aware that he had not, as yet, a great knowledge of society, he flattered himself he could tell when—and where—a young man was not wanted. There were houses in Brooklyn where such an animal was much appreciated, and there the signs were quite different They had been discouraging—except on Georgina's pail—from the first of his calling in Twelfth Street Mr. and Mrs. Gressie used to look at each other in silence when he came in, and indulge in strange, perpendicular salutations, without any shaking of hands. People did that at Portsmouth, N.H., when they were glad to see you; but in New York there was more luxuriance, and gesture had a different value. He had never, in Twelfth Street, been asked to "take anything," though the house had a delightful suggestion, a positive aroma, of sideboards,—as if there were mahogany "cellarettes" under every table. The old people, moreover, had repeatedly expressed surprise at the quantity of leisure that officers in the navy seemed to enjoy. The only way in which they had not made themselves offensive was by always remaining in the other room; though at times even this detachment, to which he owed some delightful moments, presented itself to Benyon as a form of disapprobation. Of course, after Mrs. Gressie's message, his visits were practically at an end; he would n't give the girl up, but he would n't be beholden to her father for the opportunity to converse with her. Nothing was left for the tender couple—there was a curious mutual mistrust in their tenderness—but to meet in the squares, or in the topmost streets, or in the sidemost avenues, on the afternoons of spring. It was especially during this phase of their relations that Georgina struck Benyon as imperial Her whole person seemed to exhale a tranquil, happy consciousness of having broken a law. She never told him how she arranged the matter at home, how she found it possible always to keep the appointments (to meet him out of the house) that she so boldly made, in what degree she dissimulated to her parents, and how much, in regard to their continued acquaintance, the old people suspected and accepted. If Mr. and Mrs. Gressie had forbidden him the house, it was not, apparently, because they wished her to walk with him in the Tenth Avenue or to sit at his side under the blossoming lilacs in Stuyvesant Square. He didn't believe that she told lies in Twelfth Street; he thought she was too imperial to lie; and he wondered what she said to her mother when, at the end of nearly a whole afternoon of vague peregrination with her lover, this bridling, bristling matron asked her where she had been. Georgina was capable of simply telling the truth; and yet if she simply told the truth, it was a wonder that she had not been simply packed off to Europe.

Benyon's ignorance of her pretexts is a proof that this rather oddly-mated couple never arrived at perfect intimacy,—in spite of a fact which remains to be related. He thought of this afterwards, and thought how strange it was that he had not felt more at liberty to ask her what she did for him, and how she did it, and how much she suffered for him. She would probably not have admitted that she suffered at all, and she had no wish to pose for a martyr.

Benyon remembered this, as I say, in the after years, when he tried to explain to himself certain things which simply puzzled him; it came back to him with the vision, already faded, of shabby cross-streets, straggling toward rivers, with red sunsets, seen through a haze of dust, at the end; a vista through which the figures of a young man and a girl slowly receded and disappeared,—strolling side by side, with the relaxed pace of desultory talk, but more closely linked as they passed into the distance, linked by its at last appearing safe to them—in the Tenth Avenue—that the young lady should take his arm. They were always approaching that inferior thoroughfare; but he could scarcely have told you, in those days, what else they were approaching. He had nothing in the world but his pay, and he felt that this was rather a "mean" income to offer Miss Gressie. Therefore he did n't put it forward; what he offered, instead, was the expression—crude often, and almost boyishly extravagant—of a delighted admiration of her beauty, the tenderest tones of his voice, the softest assurances of his eye and the most insinuating pressure of her hand at those moments when she consented to place it in his arm. All this was an eloquence which, if necessary, might have been condensed into a single sentence; but those few words were scarcely needful, when it was as plain that he expected—in general—she would marry him, as it was indefinite that he counted upon her for living on a few hundreds a year. If she had been a different girl he might have asked her to wait,—might have talked to her of the coming of better days, of his prospective promotion, of its being wiser, perhaps, that he should leave the navy and look about for a more lucrative career. With Georgina it was difficult to go into such questions; she had no taste whatever for detail. She was delightful as a woman to love, because when a young man is in love he discovers that; but she could not be called helpful, for she never suggested anything. That is, she never had done so till the day she really proposed—for that was the form it took—to become his wife without more delay. "Oh, yes, I will marry you;" these words, which I quoted a little way back, were not so much the answer to something he had said at the moment, as the light conclusion of a report she had just made, for the first time, of her actual situation in her father's house.

"I am afraid I shall have to see less of you," she had begun by saying. "They watch me so much."

"It is very little already," he answered. "What is once or twice a week?"

"That's easy for you to say. You are your own master, but you don't know what I go through."

"Do they make it very bad for you, dearest? Do they make scenes?" Benyon asked.

"No, of course not. Don't you know us enough to know how we behave? No scenes,—that would be a relief. However, I never make them myself, and I never will—that's one comfort for you, for the future, if you want to know. Father and mother keep very quiet, looking at me as if I were one of the lost, with hard, screwing eyes, like gimlets. To me they scarcely say anything, but they talk it all over with each other, and try and decide what is to be done. It's my belief that father has written to the people in Washington—what do you call it! the Department—to have you moved away from Brooklyn,—to have you sent to sea."

"I guess that won't do much good. They want me in Brooklyn, they don't want me at sea."

"Well, they are capable of going to Europe for a year, on purpose to take me," Geoigina said.

"How can they take you, if you won't go? And if you should go, what good would it do, if you were only to find me here when you came back, just the same as you left me?"

"Oh, well!" said Georgina, with her lovely smile, "of course they think that absence would cure me of—cure me of—" And she paused, with a certain natural modesty, not saying exactly of what.

"Cure you of what, darling? Say it, please say it," the young man murmured, drawing her hand surreptitiously into his arm.

"Of my absurd infatuation!"

"And would it, dearest?"

"Yes, very likely. But I don't mean to try. I sha'n't go to Europe,—not when I don't want to. But it's better I should see less of you,—even that I should appear—a little—to give you up."

"A little? What do you call a little?"

Georgina said nothing, for a moment. "Well, that, for instance, you should n't hold my hand quite so tight!" And she disengaged this conscious member from the pressure of his arm.

"What good will that do?" Benyon asked,

"It will make them think it 's all over,—that we have agreed to part."

"And as we have done nothing of the kind, how will that help us?"

They had stopped at the crossing of a street; a heavy dray was lumbering slowly past them. Georgina, as she stood there, turned her face to her lover, and rested her eyes for some moments on his own. At last: "Nothing will help us; I don't think we are very happy," she answered, while her strange, ironical, inconsequent smile played about her beautiful lips.

"I don't understand how you see things. I thought you were going to say you would marry me!" Benyon rejoined, standing there still, though the dray had passed.

"Oh, yes, I will marry you!" And she moved away, across the street. That was the manner in which she had said it, and it was very characteristic of her. When he saw that she really meant it, he wished they were somewhere else,—he hardly knew where the proper place would be,—so that he might take her in his arms. Nevertheless, before they separated that day he had said to her he hoped she remembered they would be very poor, reminding her how great a change she would find it She answered that she should n't mind, and presently she said that if this was all that prevented them the sooner they were married the better. The next time he saw her she was quite of the same opinion; but he found, to his surprise, it was now her conviction that she had better not leave her father's house. The ceremony should take place secretly, of course; but they would wait awhile to let their union be known.

21

"What good will it do us, then?" Raymond Benyon asked.

Georgina colored. "Well, if you don't know, I can't tell you!"

Then it seemed to him that he did know. Yet, at the same time, he could not see why, once the knot was tied, secrecy should be required. When he asked what special event they were to wait for, and what should give them the signal to appear as man and wife, she answered that her parents would probably forgive her, if they were to discover, not too abruptly, after six months, that she had taken the great step. Benyon supposed that she had ceased to care whether they forgave her or not; but he had already perceived that women are full of inconsistencies. He had believed her capable of marrying him out of bravado, but the pleasure of defiance was absent if the marriage was kept to themselves. Now, too, it appeared that she was not especially anxious to defy,—she was disposed rather to manage, to cultivate opportunities and reap the fruits of a waiting game.

"Leave it to me. Leave it to me. You are only a blundering man," Georgina said. "I shall know much better than you the right moment for saying, 'Well, you may as well make the best of it, because we have already done it!'"

That might very well be, but Benyon did n't quite understand, and he was awkwardly anxious (for a lover) till it came over him afresh that there was one thing at any rate in his favor, which was simply that the loveliest girl he had ever seen was ready to throw herself into his arms. When he said to her, "There is one thing I hate in this plan of yours,—that, for ever so few weeks, so few days, your father should support my wife,"—when he made this homely remark, with a little flush of sincerity in his face, she gave him a specimen of that unanswerable laugh of hers, and declared that it would serve Mr. Gressie right for being so barbarous and so horrid. It was Benyon's view that from the moment she disobeyed her father, she ought to cease to avail herself of his protection; but I am bound to add that he was not particularly surprised at finding this a kind of honor in which her feminine nature was little versed. To make her his wife first—at the earliest moment—whenever she would, and trust to fortune, and the new influence he should have, to give him, as soon thereafter as possible, complete possession of her,—this rather promptly presented itself to the young man as the course most worthy of a person of spirit. He would be only a pedant who would take nothing because he could not get everything at once. They wandered further than usual this afternoon, and the dusk was thick by the time he brought her back to her father's door. It was not his habit to como so near it, but to-day they had so much to talk about that he actually stood with her for ten minutes at the foot of the steps. He was keeping her hand in his, and she let it rest there while she said,—by way of a remark that should sum up all their reasons and reconcile their differences,—

"There's one great thing it will do, you know; it will make me safe."

"Safe from what?"

"From marrying any one else."

"Ah, my girl, if you were to do that—!" Benyon exclaimed; but he did n't mention the other branch of the contingency. Instead of this, he looked up at the blind face of the house—there were only dim lights in two or three windows, and no apparent eyes—and up and down the empty street, vague in the friendly twilight; after which he drew Georgina Gressie to his breast and gave her a long, passionate kiss. Yes, decidedly, he felt, they had better be married. She had run quickly up the steps, and while she stood there, with her hand on the bell, she almost hissed at him, under her breath, "Go away, go away; Amanda's coming!" Amanda was the parlor-maid, and it was in those terms that the Twelfth Street Juliet dismissed her Brooklyn Romeo. As he wandered back into the Fifth Avenue, where the evening air was conscious of a vernal fragrance from the shrubs in the little precinct of the pretty Gothic church ornamenting that charming part of the street, he was too absorbed in the impression of the delightful contact from which the girl had violently released herself to reflect that the great reason she had mentioned a moment before was a reason for their marrying, of course, but not in the least a reason for their not making it public. But, as I said in the opening lines of this chapter, if he did not understand his mistress's motives at the end, he cannot be expected to have understood them at the beginning.

II.

Mrs. Portico, as we know, was always talking about going to Europe; but she had not yet—I mean a year after the incident I have just related—put her hand upon a youthful cicerone. Petticoats, of course, were required; it was necessary that her companion should be of the sex which sinks most naturally upon benches, in galleries and cathredrals, and pauses most frequently upon staircases that ascend to celebrated views. She was a widow, with a good fortune and several sons, all of whom were in Wall Street, and none of them capable of the relaxed pace at which she expected to take her foreign tour. They were all in a state of tension. They went through life standing. She was a short, broad, high-colored woman, with a loud voice, and superabundant black hair, arranged in a way peculiar to herself,—with so many combs and bands that it had the appearance of a national coiffure. There was an impression in New York, about 1845, that the style was Danish; some one had said something about having seen it in Schleswig-Holstein.

Mrs. Portico had a bold, humorous, slightly flamboyant look; people who saw her for the first time received an impression that her late husband had married the daughter of a barkeeper or the proprietress of a menageria. Her high, hoarse, good-natured voice seemed to connect her in some way with public life; it was not pretty enough to suggest that she might have been an actress. These ideas quickly passed away, however, even if you were not sufficiently initiated to know—as all the Grossies, for instance, knew so well—that her origin, so far from being enveloped in mystery, was almost the sort of thing she might have boasted of. But in spite of the high pitch of her appearance, she didn't boast of anything; she was a genial, easy, comical, irreverent person, with a large charity, a democratic, fraternizing turn of mind, and a contempt for many worldly standards, which she expressed not in the least in general axioms (for she had a mortal horror of philosophy), but in violent ejaculations on particular occasions. She had not a grain of moral timidity, and she fronted a delicate social problem as sturdily as she would have barred the way of a gentleman she might have met in her vestibule with the plate-chest The only thing which prevented her being a bore in orthodox circles was that she was incapable of discussion. She never lost her temper, but she lost her vocabulary, and ended quietly by praying that Heaven would give her an opportunity to *show* what she believed.

She was an old friend of Mr. and Mrs. Gressie, who esteemed her for the antiquity of her lineage and the frequency of her subscriptions, and to whom she rendered the service of making them feel liberal,—like people too sure of their own position to be frightened. She was their indulgence, their dissipation, their point of contact with dangerous heresies; so long as they continued to see her they could not be accused of being narrow-minded,—a matter as to which they were perhaps vaguely conscious of the necessity of taking their precautions. Mrs. Portico never asked herself whether she liked the Gressies; she had no disposition for morbid analysis, she accepted transmitted associations, and she found, somehow, that her acquaintance with these people helped her to relieve herself. She was always making scenes in their drawing-room, scenes half indignant, half jocose, like all her manifestations, to which it must be confessed that they adapted themselves beautifully. They never "met" her in the language of controversy; but always collected to watch her, with smiles and comfortable platitudes, as if they envied her superior richness of temperament She took an interest in Georgina, who seemed to her different from the others, with suggestions about her of being likely not to marry so unrefreshingly as her sisters had done, and of a high, bold standard of duty. Her sisters had married from duty, but Mrs. Portico would rather have chopped off one of her large, plump hands than behave herself so well as that She had, in her daughterless condition, a certain ideal of a girl that should be beautiful and romantic, with lustrous eyes, and a little persecuted, so that she, Mrs. Portico, might get her out of her troubles. She looked to Georgina, to a considerable degree, to gratify her in this way; but she had really never understood Geoigina at all She ought to have been shrewd, but she lacked this refinement, and she never understood anything until after many disappointments and vexations. It was difficult to startle her, but she was much startled by a communication that this young lady made her one fine spring morning. With her florid appearance and her speculative mind, she was probably the most innocent woman in New York.

Georgina came very early,—earlier even than visits were paid in New York thirty years ago; and instantly, without any preface, looking her straight in the face, told Mrs. Portico that she was in great trouble and must appeal to her for assistance. Georgina had in her aspect no symptom of distress; she was as fresh and beautiful as the April day itself; she held up her head and smiled, with a sort of familiar bravado, looking like a young woman who would naturally be on good terms with fortune. It was not in the least in the tone of a person making a confession or relating a misadventure that she presently said: "Well, you must know, to begin with—of course, it will surprise you—that I 'm married."

"Married, Georgina Grossie!" Mrs. Portico repeated in her most resonant tones.

Georgina got up, walked with her majestic step across the room, and closed the door. Then she stood there, her back pressed against the mahogany panels, indicating only by the distance she had placed between herself and her hostess the consciousness of an irregular position. "I am not Georgina Gressie! I am Georgina Benyon,—and it has become plain, within a short time, that the natural consequence will take place."

Mrs. Portico was altogether bewildered. "The natural consequence?" she exclaimed, staring.

"Of one's being married, of course,—I suppose you know what that is. No one must know anything about it. I want you to take me to Europe."

Mrs. Portico now slowly rose from her place, and approached her visitor, looking at her from head to foot as she did so, as if to challenge the truth of her remarkable announcement. She rested her hands on Georgina's shoulders a moment, gazing into her blooming face, and then she drew her closer and kissed her. In this way the girl was conducted back to the sofa, where, in a conversation of extreme intimacy, she opened Mrs. Portico's eyes wider than they had ever been opened before. She was Raymond Benyon's wife; they had been married a year, but no one knew anything about it. She had kept it from every one, and she meant to go on keeping it. The ceremony had taken place in a little Episcopal church at Harlem, one Sunday afternoon, after the service.

There was no one in that dusty suburb who knew them; the clergyman, vexed at being detained, and wanting to go home to tea, had made no trouble; he tied the knot before they could turn round. It was ridiculous how easy it had been. Raymond had told him frankly that it must all be under the rose, as the young lady's family disapproved of what she was doing. But she was of legal age, and perfectly free; he could see that for himself. The parson had given a grunt as he looked at her over his spectacles. It was not very complimentary; it seemed to say that she was indeed no chicken. Of course she looked old for a girl; but she was not a girl now, was she? Raymond had certified his own identity as an officer in the United States Navy (he had papers, besides his uniform, which he wore), and introduced the clergyman to a friend he had brought with him, who was also in the navy, a venerable paymaster. It was he who gave Georgina away, as it were; he was an old, old man, a regular grandmother, and perfectly safe. He had been married three times himself. After the ceremony she went back to her father's; but she saw Mr. Benyon the next day. After that, she saw him—for a little while—pretty often. He was always begging her to come to him altogether; she must do him that justice. But she wouldn't—she wouldn't now—perhaps she would n't ever. She had her reasons, which seemed to her very good, but were very difficult to explain. She would tell Mrs. Portico in plenty of time what they were. But that was not the question now, whether they were good or bad; the question was for her to get away from the country for several months,—far away from any one who had ever known her. She would like to go to some little place in Spain or Italy, where she should be out of the world until everything was over.

Mrs. Portico's heart gave a jump as this serene, handsome, familiar girl, sitting there with a hand in hers, and pouring forth this extraordinary tale, spoke of everything being over. There was a glossy coldness in it, an unnatural lightness, which suggested—poor Mrs. Portico scarcely knew what. If Georgina was to become a mother, it was to be supposed she was to remain a mother. She said there was a beautiful place in Italy—Genoa—of which Raymond had often spoken—and where he had been more than once,—he admired it so much; could n't they go there and be quiet for a little while? She was asking a great favor,—that she knew very well; but if Mrs. Portico would n't take her, she would find some one who would. They had talked of such a journey so often; and, certainly, if Mrs. Portico had been willing before, she ought to be much more willing now. The girl declared that she must do something,—go somewhere,—keep, in one way or another, her situation unperceived. There was no use talking to her about telling,—she would rather die than tell. No doubt it seemed strange, but she knew what she was about. No one had guessed anything yet,—she had succeeded perfectly in doing what she wished,—and her father and mother believed—as Mrs. Portico had believed,—had n't she?—that, any time the last year, Raymond Beuyon was less to her than he had been before. Well, so he was; yes, he was. He had gone away—he was off, Heaven knew where—in the Pacific; she was alone, and now she would remain alone. The family believed it was all over,—with his going back to his ship, and other things, and they were right: for it *was* over, or it would be soon.

Mrs. Portico, by this time, had grown almost afraid of her young friend; *she* had so little fear, she had even, as it were, so little shame. If the good lady had been accustomed to analyzing things a little more, she would have said she had so little conscience. She looked at Georgina with dilated eyes,—her visitor was so much the calmer of the two,—and exclaimed, and murmured, and sunk back, and sprung forward, and wiped her forehead with her pocket-handkerchief! There were things she didn't understand; that they should all have been so deceived, that they should have thought Georgina was giving her lover up (they flattered themselves she was discouraged, or had grown tired of him), when she was really only making it impossible she should belong to any one else. And with this, her inconsequence, her capriciousness, her absence of motive, the way she contradicted herself, her apparent belief that she could hush up such a situation forever! There was nothing shameful in having married poor Mr. Benyon, even in a little church at Harlem, and being given away by a paymaster. It was much more shameful to be in such a state without being prepared to make the proper explanations. And she must have seen very little of her husband; she must have given him up—so far as meeting him went—almost as soon as she had taken him. Had not Mrs. Gressie herself told Mrs. Portico (in the preceding October, it must have been) that there now would be no need of sending Georgina away, inasmuch as the affair with the little navy man—a project in every way so unsuitable— had quite blown over?

"After our marriage I saw him less, I saw him a great deal less," Georgina explained; but her explanation only appeared to make the mystery more dense.

"I don't see, in that case, what on earth you married him for!"

"We had to be more careful; I wished to appear to have given him up. Of course we were really more intimate,—I saw him differently," Georgina said, smiling.

"I should think so! I can't for the life of me see why you were n't discovered."

"All I can say is we weren't No doubt it's remarkable. We managed very well,—that is, I managed,—he did n't want to manage at all. And then, father and mother are incredibly stupid!"

Mrs. Portico exhaled a comprehensive moan, feeling glad, on the whole, that she had n't a daughter, while Georgina went on to furnish a few more details. Raymond Benyon, in the summer, had been ordered from Brooklyn to Charlestown, near Boston, where, as Mrs. Portico perhaps knew, there was another navy-yard, in which there was a temporary press of work, requiring more oversight He had remained there several months, during which he had written to her urgently to come to him, and during which, as well, he had received notice that he was to rejoin his ship a little later. Before doing so he came back to Brooklyn for a few weeks to wind up his work there, and then she had seen him—well, pretty often. That was the best time of all the year that had elapsed since their marriage. It was a wonder at home that nothing had then been guessed; because she had really been reckless, and Benyon had even tried to force on a disclosure. But they *were* stupid, that was very certain. He had besought her again and again to put an end to their false position, but she did n't want it any more than she had wanted it before. They had rather a bad parting; in fact, for a pair of lovers, it was a very queer parting indeed. He did n't know, now, the thing she had come to tell Mrs. Portico. She had not written to him. He was on a very long cruise. It might be two years before he returned to the United States. "I don't care how long he stays away," Georgina said, very simply.

"You haven't mentioned why you married him. Perhaps you don't remember," Mrs. Portico broke out, with her masculine laugh.

"Oh, yes; I loved him!"

"And you have got over that?"

Georgina hesitated a moment. "Why, no, Mrs. Portico, of course I haven't; Raymond's a splendid fellow."

"Then why don't you live with him? You don't explain that."

"What would be the use when he's always away? How can one live with a man that spends half his life in the South Seas? If he was n't in the navy it would be different; but to go through everything,—I mean everything that making our marriage known would bring upon me,—the scolding and the exposure and the ridicule, the scenes at home,—to go through it all, just for the idea, and yet be alone here, just as I was before, without my husband after all,—with none of the good of him,"—and here Georgina looked at her hostess as if with the certitude that such an enumeration of inconveniences would touch her effectually,—"really, Mrs. Portico, I am bound to say I don't think that would be worth while; I haven't the courage for it."

"I never thought you were a coward," said Mrs. Portico.

"Well, I am not,—if you will give me time. I am very patient."

"I never thought that, either."

"Marrying changes one," said Georgina, still smiling.

"It certainly seems to have had a very peculiar effect upon you. Why don't you make him leave the navy, and arrange your life comfortably, like every one else?"

"I would n't for the world interfere with his prospects—with his promotion. That is sure to come for him, and to come quickly, he has such talents. He is devoted to his profession; it would ruin him to leave it."

"My dear young woman, you are a wonderful creature!" Mrs. Portico exclaimed, looking at her companion as if she had been in a glass case.

"So poor Raymond says," Georgina answered, smiling more than ever.

"Certainly, I should have been very sorry to marry a navy man; but if I had married him, I should stick to him, in the face of all the scoldings in the universe!"

"I don't know what your parents may have been; I know what mine are,", Georgina replied, with some dignity. "When he's a captain, we shall come out of hiding."

"And what shall you do meanwhile? What will you do with your children? Where will you hide them? What will you do with this one?"

Georgina rested her eyes on her lap for a minute; then, raising them, she met those of Mrs. Portico. "Somewhere in Europe," she said, in her sweet tone.

"Georgina Gressie, you 're a monster!" the elder lady cried.

"I know what I am about, and you will help me," the girl went on.

"I will go and tell your father and mother the whole story,—that's what I will do!"

"I am not in the least afraid of that, not in the least. You will help me,—I assure you that you will."

"Do you mean I will support the child?"

Georgina broke into a laugh. "I do believe you would, if I were to ask you! But I won't go so far as that; I have something of my own. All I want you to do is to be with me."

"At Genoa,—yes, you have got it all fixed! You say Mr. Benyon is so fond of the place. That's all very well; but how will he like his infant being deposited there?"

"He won't like it at all. You see I tell you the whole truth," said Georgina, gently.

31

"Much obliged; it's a pity you keep it all for me! It is in his power, then, to make you behave properly. *He* can publish your marriage if you won't; and if he does you will have to acknowledge your child."

"Publish, Mrs. Portico? How little you know my Raymond! He will never break a promise; he will go through fire first."

"And what have you got him to promise?"

"Never to insist on a disclosure against my will; never to claim me openly as his wife till I think it is time; never to let any one know what has passed between us if I choose to keep it still a secret—to keep it for years—to keep it forever. Never to do anything in the matter himself, but to leave it to me. For this he has given me his solemn word of honor. And I know what that means!"

Mrs. Portico, on the sofa, fairly bounded.

"You *do* know what you are about And Mr. Benyon strikes me as more fantastic even than yourself. I never heard of a man taking such an imbecile vow. What good can it do him?"

"What good? The good it did him was that, it gratified me. At the time he took it he would have made any promise under the sun. It was a condition I exacted just at the very last, before the marriage took place. There was nothing at that moment he would have refused me; there was nothing I could n't have made him do. He was in love to that degree—but I don't want to boast," said Georgina, with quiet grandeur. "He wanted—he wanted—" she added; but then she paused.

"He does n't seem to have wanted much!" Mrs. Portico cried, in a tone which made Georgina turn to the window, as if it might have reached the street.

Her hostess noticed the movement and went on: "Oh, my dear, if I ever do tell your story, I will tell it so that people will hear it!"

"You never will tell it. What I mean is, that Raymond wanted the sanction—of the affair at the church—because he saw that I would never do without it. Therefore, for him, the sooner we had it the better, and, to hurry it on, he was ready to take any pledge."

"You have got it pat enough," said Mrs. Portico, in homely phrase. "I don't know what you mean by sanctions, or what *you* wanted of 'em!"

Georgina got up, holding rather higher than before that beautiful head which, in spite of the embarrassments of this interview, had not yet perceptibly abated of its elevation. "Would you have liked me to—to not marry?"

Mrs. Portico rose also, and, flushed with the agitation of unwonted knowledge,—it was as if she had discovered a skeleton in her favorite cupboard,—faced her young friend for a moment. Then her conflicting sentiments resolved themselves into an abrupt question, uttered,—for Mrs. Portico,—with much solemnity: "Georgina Gressie, were you really in love with him?"

The question suddenly dissipated the girl's strange, studied, wilful coldness; she broke out, with a quick flash of passion,—a passion that, for the moment, was predominantly anger, "Why else, in Heaven's name, should I have done what I have done? Why else should I have married him? What under the sun had I to gain?"

A certain quiver in Georgina's voice, a light in her eye which seemed to Mrs. Portico more spontaneous, more human, as she uttered these words, caused them to affect her hostess rather less painfully than anything she had yet said. She took the girl's hand and emitted indefinite, admonitory sounds. "Help me, my dear old friend, help me," Georgina continued, in a low, pleading tone; and in a moment Mrs. Portico saw that the tears were in her eyes.

"You 're a queer mixture, my child," she exclaimed. "Go straight home to your own mother, and tell her everything; that is your best help."

"You are kinder than my mother. You must n't judge her by yourself."

"What can she do to you? How can she hurt you? We are not living in pagan times," said Mrs. Portico, who was seldom so historical "Besides,

33

you have no reason to speak of your mother—to think of her, even—so! She would have liked you to marry a man of some property; but she has always been a good mother to you."

At this rebuke Georgina suddenly kindled again; she was, indeed, as Mrs. Portico had said, a queer mixture. Conscious, evidently, that she could not satisfactorily justify her present stiffness, she wheeled round upon a grievance which absolved her from self-defence. "Why, then, did he make that promise, if he loved me? No man who really loved me would have made it,—and no man that was a man, as I understand being a man! He might have seen that I only did it to test him,—to see if he wanted to take advantage of being left free himself. It is a proof that he does n't love me,—not as he ought to have done; and in such a case as that a woman is n't bound to make sacrifices!"

Mrs. Portico was not a person of a nimble intellect; her mind moved vigorously, but heavily; yet she sometimes made happy guesses. She saw that Georgia's emotions were partly real and partly fictitious; that, as regards this last matter, especially, she was trying to "get up" a resentment, in order to excuse herself. The pretext was absurd, and the good lady was struck with its being heartless on the part of her young visitor to reproach poor Benyon with a concession on which she had insisted, and which could only be a proof of his devotion, inasmuch as he left her free while he bound himself. Altogether, Mrs. Portico was shocked and dismayed at such a want of simplicity in the behavior of a young person whom she had hitherto believed to be as candid as she was elegant, and her appreciation of this discovery expressed itself in the uncompromising remark: "You strike me as a very bad girl, my dear; you strike me as a very bad girl!"

PART II.

III.

It will doubtless seem to the reader very singular that, in spite of this reflection, which appeared to sum up her judgment of the matter, Mrs. Portico should, in the course of a very few days, have consented to everything that Georgina asked of her. I have thought it well to narrate at length the first conversation that took place between them, but I shall not trace further the details of the girl's hard pleading, or the steps by which—in the face of a hundred robust and salutary convictions—the loud, kind, sharp, simple, sceptical, credulous woman took under her protection a damsel whose obstinacy she could not speak of without getting red with anger. It was the simple fact of Georgina's personal condition that moved her; this young lady's greatest eloquence was the seriousness of her predicament She might be bad, and she had a splendid, careless, insolent, fair-faced way of admitting it, which at moments, incoherently, inconsistently, and irresistibly, resolved the harsh confession into tears of weakness; but Mrs. Portico had known her from her rosiest years, and when Georgina declared that she could n't go home, that she wished to be with her and not with her mother, that she could n't expose herself,—how could she?—and that she must remain with her and her only till the day they should sail, the poor lady was forced to make that day a reality. She was overmastered, she was cajoled, she was, to a certain extent, fascinated. She had to accept Georgina's rigidity (she had none of her own to oppose to it; she was only violent, she was not continuous), and once she did this, it was plain, after all, that to take her young friend to Europe was to help her, and to leave her alone was not to help her. Georgina literally frightened Mrs. Portico into compliance. She was evidently capable of strange things if thrown upon her own devices.

So, from one day to another Mrs. Portico announced that she was really at last about to sail for foreign lands (her doctor having told her that if she did n't look out she would get too old to enjoy them), and that she had invited that robust Miss Gressie, who could stand so long on her feet, to accompany her. There was joy in the house of Gressie at this announcement, for though the danger was over, it was a great general advantage to Georgina to go, and the Gressies were always elated at the prospect of an advantage. There was a danger that she might meet Mr. Benyon on the other side of the world; but it didn't seem likely that Mrs. Portico would lend herself to a plot of that kind. If she had taken it into her head to favor their love affair, she would have done it frankly, and Georgina would have been married by this time. Her arrangements were made as quickly as her decision had been—or rather had appeared—slow; for this concerned those agile young men down town. Georgina was perpetually at her house; it was understood in Twelfth Street that she was talking over her future travels with her kind friend. Talk there was, of course to a considerable degree; but after it was settled they should start nothing more was said about the motive of the journey. Nothing was said, that is, till the night before they sailed; then a few words passed between them. Georgina had already taken leave of her relations in Twelfth Street, and was to sleep at Mrs. Portico's in order to go down to the ship at an early hour. The two ladies were sitting together in the firelight, silent, with the consciousness of corded luggage, when the elder one suddenly remarked to her companion that she seemed to be taking a great deal upon herself in assuming that Raymond Benyon wouldn't force her hand. *He* might choose to acknowledge his child, if she didn't; there were promises and promises, and many people would consider they had been let off when circumstances were so altered. She would have to reckon with Mr. Benyon more than she thought.

"I know what I am about," Georgina answered. "There is only one promise, for him. I don't know what you mean by circumstances being altered."

"Everything seems to me to be changed," poor Mrs. Portico murmured, rather tragically.

"Well, he is n't, and he never will! I am sure of him,—as sure as that I sit here. Do you think I would have looked at him if I had n't known he was a man of his word?"

"You have chosen him well, my dear," said Mrs. Portico, who by this time was reduced to a kind of bewildered acquiescence.

"Of course I have chosen him well! In such a matter as this he will be perfectly splendid." Then suddenly, "Perfectly splendid,—that's why I cared for him!" she repeated, with a flash of incongruous passion.

This seemed to Mrs. Portico audacious to the point of being sublime; but she had given up trying to understand anything that the girl might say or do. She understood less and less, after they had disembarked in England and begun to travel southward; and she understood least of all when, in the middle of the winter, the event came off with which, in imagination, she had tried to familiarize herself, but which, when it occurred, seemed to her beyond measure strange and dreadful. It took place at Genoa, for Georgina had made up her mind that there would be more privacy in a big town than in a little; and she wrote to America that both Mrs. Portico and she had fallen in love with the place and would spend two or three months there. At that time people in the United States knew much less than to-day about the comparative attractions of foreign cities, and it was not thought surprising that absent New Yorkers should wish to linger in a seaport where they might find apartments, according to Georgina's report, in a palace painted in fresco by Vandyke and Titian. Georgina, in her letters, omitted, it will be seen, no detail that could give color to Mrs. Portico's long stay at Genoa. In such a palace—where the travellers hired twenty gilded rooms for the most insignificant sum—a remarkably fine boy came into the world. Nothing could have been more successful and comfortable than this transaction. Mrs. Portico was almost appalled at the facility and felicity of it. She was by this time in a pretty bad way, and—what had never happened to her before in her life—she suffered from chronic depression of spirits. She hated to have to lie, and now she was lying all the time. Everything she wrote home, everything that had been said or done in connection with their stay in Genoa, was a lie. The way they remained indoors to avoid meeting chance compatriots was a lie. Compatriots, in Genoa, at that period, were very rare; but nothing could exceed the businesslike completeness of Georgina's precautions. Her nerves, her self-possession, her apparent want of feeling, excited on Mrs. Portico's part a kind of gloomy suspense; a morbid anxiety to see how far her companion would go took possession of the excellent woman, who, a few months before, hated to fix her mind on disagreeable things.

Georgina went very far indeed; she did everything in her power to dissimulate the origin of her child. The record of its birth was made under a false name, and he was baptized at the nearest church by a Catholic priest. A magnificent contadina was brought to light by the doctor in a village in the hills, and this big, brown, barbarous creature, who, to do her justice, was full of handsome, familiar smiles and coarse tenderness, was constituted nurse to Raymond Benyon's son. She nursed him for a fortnight under the mother's eye, and she was then sent back to her village with the baby in her arms and sundry gold coin knotted into a corner of her rude pocket-handkerchief. Mr. Gressie had given his daughter a liberal letter of credit on a London banker, and she was able, for the present, to make abundant provision for the little one. She called Mrs. Portico's attention to the fact that she spent none of her money on futilities; she kept it all for her small pensioner in the Genoese hills. Mrs. Portico beheld these strange doings with a stupefaction that occasionally broke into passionate protest; then she relapsed into a brooding sense of having now been an accomplice so far that she must be an accomplice to the end. The two ladies went down to Rome—Georgina was in wonderful trim—to finish the season, and here Mrs. Portico became convinced that she intended to abandon her offspring. She had not driven into the country to see the nursling before leaving Genoa,—she had said that she could n't bear to see it in such a place and among such people. Mrs. Portico, it must be added, had felt the force of this plea,—felt it as regards a plan of her own, given up after being hotly entertained for a few hours, of devoting a day, by herself, to a visit to the big contadina. It seemed to her that if she should see the child in the sordid hands to which Georgina had consigned it she would become still more of a participant than she was already. This young woman's blooming hardness, after they got to Borne, acted upon her like a kind of Medusa-mask. She had seen a horrible thing, she had been mixed up with it, and her motherly heart had received a mortal chill. It became more clear to her every day that, though Georgina would continue to send the infant money in considerable quantities, she had dispossessed herself of it forever. Together with this induction a fixed idea settled in her mind,—the project of taking the baby herself, of making him her own, of arranging that matter with the father. The countenance she had given Georgina up to this point was an effective pledge that she would not expose her; but she could adopt the child without exposing her; she could say that he was a lovely baby—he was lovely, fortunately—whom she had picked up in a poor village in Italy,—a village that had been devastated by brigands. She would pretend—she could pretend; oh, yes, of course, she could pretend! Everything was imposture now, and she could go on to lie as she had begun. The falsity of the whole business sickened her; it made her so yellow that she scarcely knew herself in her glass. None the less, to rescue the child, even if she had to become falser still, would be in some measure an atonement for the treachery to which she had already lent herself. She began to hate Georgina, who had drawn her into such an atrocious current, and if it had not been for two considerations she would have insisted on their separating. One was the deference she owed to Mr. and Mrs. Gressie, who had reposed such a trust in her; the other was that she must keep hold of the mother till she had got possession of the infant Meanwhile, in this forced communion, her aversion to her companion increased; Georgina came to appear to her a creature of brass, of iron; she was exceedingly afraid of her, and it seemed to her now a wonder of wonders that she should ever have trusted her enough to come so far. Georgina showed no consciousness of the change in Mrs. Portico, though there was, indeed, at present, not even a pretence of confidence between the two. Miss Gressie—that was another lie, to which Mrs. Portico had to lend herself—was bent on enjoying Europe, and was especially delighted with Rome. She certainly had the courage of her undertaking, and she confessed to Mrs. Portico that she had left Raymond Benyon, and meant to continue to leave him, in ignorance of what had taken place at Genoa. There was a certain confidence, it must be said, in that. He was now in Chinese waters, and she probably should not see him for years.

Mrs. Portico took counsel with herself, and the result of her cogitation was, that she wrote to Mr. Benyon that a charming little boy had been born to him, and that Georgina had put him to nurse with Italian peasants, but that, if he would kindly consent to it, she, Mrs. Portico, would bring him up much better than that. She knew not how to address her letter, and Georgina, even if *she* should know, which was doubtful, would never tell her; so she sent the missive to the care of the Secretary of the Navy, at Washington, with an earnest request that it might immediately be forwarded. Such was Mrs. Portico's last effort in this strange business of Georgina's. I relate rather a complicated fact in a very few words when I say that the poor lady's anxieties, indignations, repentances, preyed upon her until they fairly broke her down. Various persons whom she knew in Borne notified her that the air of the Seven Hills was plainly unfavorable to her, and she had made up her mind to return to her native land, when she found that, in her depressed condition, malarial fever had laid its hand upon her. She was unable to move, and the matter was settled for her in the course of an illness which, happily, was not prolonged. I have said that she was not obstinate, and the resistance that she made on the present occasion was not worthy even of her spasmodic energy. Brain-fever made its appearance, and she died at the end of three weeks, during which Georgina's attentions to her patient and protectress had been unremitting. There were other Americans in Rome who, after this sad event, extended to the bereaved young lady every comfort and hospitality. She had no lack of opportunities for returning under a proper escort to New York. She selected, you may be sure, the best, and re-entered her father's house, where she took to plain dressing; for she sent all her pocket-money, with the utmost secrecy, to the little boy in the Genoese hills.

IV.

"Why should he come if he doesn't like you? He is under no obligation, and he has his ship to look after. Why should he sit for an hour at a time, and why should he be so pleasant?"

"Do you think he is very pleasant?" Kate Theory asked, turning away her face from her sister. It was important that Mildred should not see how little the expression of that charming countenance corresponded with the inquiry.

This precaution was useless, however, for in a moment Mildred said, from the delicately draped couch, where she lay at the open window, "Kate Theory, don't be affected!"

"Perhaps it's for you he comes. I don't see why he should n't; you are far more attractive than I, and you have a great deal more to say. How can he help seeing that you are the cleverest of the clever? You can talk to him of everything: of the dates of the different eruptions, of the statues and bronzes in the Museum, which you have never seen, poor darling! but which you know more about than he does, than any one does. What was it you began on last time? Oh, yes, you poured forth floods about Magna Græcia. And then—and then—" But with this Kate Theory paused; she felt it would n't do to speak the words that had risen to her lips. That her sister was as beautiful as a saint, and as delicate and refined as an angel,—she had been on the point of saying something of that sort But Mildred's beauty and delicacy were the fairness of mortal disease, and to praise her for her refinement was simply to intimate that she had the tenuity of a consumptive. So, after she had checked herself, the younger girl—she was younger only by a year or two—simply kissed her tenderly, and settled the knot of the lace handkerchief that was tied over her head. Mildred knew what she had been going to say,—knew why she had stopped. Mildred knew everything, without ever leaving her room, or leaving, at least, that little salon of their own, at the *pension*, which she had made so pretty by simply lying there, at the window that had the view of the bay and of Vesuvius, and telling Kate how to arrange and rearrange everything. Since it began to be plain that Mildred must spend her small remnant of years altogether in warm climates, the lot of the two sisters had been cast in the ungarnished hostelries of southern Europe. Their little sitting-room was sure to be very ugly, and Mildred was never happy till it was rearranged. Her sister fell to work, as a matter of course, the first day, and changed the place of all the tables, sofas, chairs, till every combination had been tried, and the invalid thought at last that there was a little effect Kate Theory had a taste of her own, and her ideas were not always the same as her sister's; but she did whatever Mildred liked, and if the poor girl had told her to put the doormat on the dining-table, or the clock under the sofa, she would have obeyed without a murmur. Her own ideas, her personal tastes, had been folded

41

up and put away, like garments out of season, in drawers and trunks, with camphor and lavender. They were not, as a general thing, for southern wear, however indispensable to comfort in the climate of New England, where poor Mildred had lost her health. Kate Theory, ever since this event, had lived for her companion, and it was almost an inconvenience for her to think that she was attractive to Captain Benyon. It was as if she had shut up her house and was not in a position to entertain. So long as Mildred should live, her own life was suspended; if there should be any time afterwards, perhaps she would take it up again; but for the present, in answer to any knock at her door, she could only call down from one of her dusty windows that she was not at home. Was it really in these terms she should have to dismiss Captain Benyon? If Mildred said it was for her he came she must perhaps take upon herself such a duty; for, as we have seen, Mildred knew everything, and she must therefore be right She knew about the statues in the Museum, about the excavations at Pompeii, about the antique splendor of Magna Græcia. She always had some instructive volume on the table beside her sofa, and she had strength enough to hold the book for half an hour at a time. That was about the only strength she had now. The Neapolitan winters had been remarkably soft, but after the first month or two she had been obliged to give up her little walks in the garden. It lay beneath her window like a single enormous bouquet; as early as May, that year, the flowers were so dense. None of them, however, had a color so intense as the splendid blue of the bay, which filled up all the rest of the view. It would have looked painted, if you had not been able to see the little movement of the waves. Mildred Theory watched them by the hour, and the breathing crest of the volcano, on the other side of Naples, and the great sea-vision of Capri, on the horizon, changing its tint while her eyes rested there, and wondered what would become of her sister after she was gone. Now that Percival was married,—he was their only brother, and from one day to the other was to come down to Naples to show them his new wife, as yet a complete stranger, or revealed only in the few letters she had written them during her wedding tour,—now that Percival was to be quite taken up, poor Kate's situation would be much more grave. Mildred felt that she should be able to judge better, after she should have seen her sister-in-law, how much of a home Kate might expect to find with the pair; but even if Agnes should prove—well, more satisfactory than her letters, it was a wretched prospect for Kate,—this living as a mere appendage to happier people. Maiden aunts were very well, but being a maiden aunt was only a last resource, and Kate's first resources had not even been tried.

Meanwhile the latter young lady wondered as well,—wondered in what book Mildred had read that Captain Benyon was in love with her. She admired him, she thought, but he didn't seem a man that would fall in love with one like that She could see that he was on his guard; he would n't throw himself away. He thought too much of himself, or at any rate he took too good care of himself,—in the manner of a man to whom something had happened which had given him a lesson. Of course what had happened was that his heart was buried somewhere,—in some woman's grave; he had loved some beautiful girl,—much more beautiful, Kate was sure, than she, who thought herself small and dark,—and the maiden had died, and his capacity to love had died with her. He loved her memory,—that was the only thing he would care for now. He was quiet, gentle, clever, humorous, and very kind in his manner; but if any one save Mildred had said to her that if he came three times a week to Posilippo, it was for anything but to pass his time (he had told them he didn't know another soul in Naples), she would have felt that this was simply the kind of thing—usually so idiotic—that people always thought it necessary to say. It was very easy for him to come; he had the big ship's boat, with nothing else to do; and what could be more delightful than to be rowed across the bay, under a bright awning, by four brown sailors with "Louisiana" in blue letters on their immaculate white shirts, and in gilt letters on their fluttering hat ribbons? The boat came to the steps of the garden of the *pension*, where the orange-trees hung over and made vague yellow balls shine back out of the water. Kate Theory knew all about that, for Captain Benyon had persuaded her to take a turn in the boat, and if they had only had another lady to go with them, he could have conveyed her to the ship, and shown her all over it It looked beautiful, just a little way off, with the American flag hanging loose in the Italian air. They would have another lady when Agnes should arrive; then Percival would remain with Mildred while they took this excursion. Mildred had stayed alone the day she went in the boat; she had insisted on it, and, of course it was really Mildred who had

43

persuaded her; though now that Kate came to think of it, Captain Benyon had, in his quiet, waiting way—he turned out to be waiting long after you thought he had let a thing pass—said a good deal about the pleasure it would give him. Of course, everything would give pleasure to a man who was so bored. He was keeping the "Louisiana" at Naples, week after week, simply because these were the commodore's orders. There was no work to be done there, and his time was on his hands; but of course the commodore, who had gone to Constantinople with the two other ships, had to be obeyed to the letter, however mysterious his motives. It made no difference that he was a fantastic, grumbling, arbitrary old commodore; only a good while afterwards it occurred to Kate Theory that, for a reserved, correct man, Captain Benyon had given her a considerable proof of confidence, in speaking to her in these terms of his superior officer. If he looked at all hot when he arrived at the *pension*, she offered him a glass of cold "orangeade." Mildred thought this an unpleasant drink,—she called it messy; but Kate adored it, and Captain Benyon always accepted it.

The day I speak of, to change the subject, she called her sister's attention to the extraordinary sharpness of a zigzagging cloud-shadow, on the tinted slope of Vesuvius; but Mildred only remarked in answer that she wished her sister would many the captain. It was in this familiar way that constant meditation led Miss Theory to speak of him; it shows how constantly she thought of him, for, in general, no one was more ceremonious than she, and the failure of her health had not caused her to relax any form that it was possible to keep up. There was a kind of slim erectness, even in the way she lay on her sofa; and she always received the doctor as if he were calling for the first time.

"I had better wait till he asks me," Kate Theory said. "Dear Milly, if I were to do some of the things you wish me to do, I should shock you very much."

"I wish he would marry you, then. You know there is very little time, if I wish to see it."

"You will never see it, Mildred. I don't see why you should take so for granted that I would accept him."

"You will never meet a man who has so few disagreeable qualities. He is probably not enormously rich. I don't know what is the pay of a captain in the navy—"

"It's a relief to find there is something you don't know," Kate Theory broke in.

"But when I am gone," her sister went on calmly, "when I am gone there will be plenty for both of you."

The younger sister, at this, was silent for a moment; then she exclaimed, "Mildred, you may be out of health, but I don't see why you should be dreadful!"

"You know that since we have been leading this life we have seen no one we liked better," said Milly. When she spoke of the life they were leading—there was always a soft resignation of regret and contempt in the allusion—she meant the southern winters, the foreign climates, the vain experiments, the lonely waitings, the wasted hours, the interminable rains, the bad food, the pottering, humbugging doctors, the damp *pensions*, the chance encounters, the fitful apparitions, of fellow-travellers.

"Why should n't you speak for yourself alone? I am glad *you* like him, Mildred."

"If you don't like him, why do you give him orangeade?"

At this inquiry Kate began to laugh, and her sister continued,—

"Of course you are glad I like him, my dear. If I did n't like him, and you did, it would n't be satisfactory at all. I can imagine nothing more miserable; I should n't die in any sort of comfort."

Kate Theory usually checked this sort of allusion—she was always too late—with a kiss; but on this occasion she added that it was a long time since Mildred had tormented her so much as she had done to-day. "You will make me hate him," she added.

"Well, that proves you don't already," Milly rejoined; and it happened that almost at this moment they saw, in the golden afternoon, Captain Benyon's boat approaching the steps at the end of the garden. He came that day, and he came two days later, and he came yet once again after an interval equally brief, before Percival Theory arrived, with Mrs. Percival, from Borne. He seemed anxious to crowd into these few days, as he would have said, a good deal of intercourse with the two remarkably nice girls—or nice women, he hardly knew which to call them—whom in the course of a long, idle, rather tedious detention at Naples, he had discovered in the lovely suburb of Posilippo. It was the American consul who had put him into relation with them; the sisters had had to sign, in the consul's presence, some law-papers, transmitted to them by the man of business who looked after their little property in America, and the kindly functionary, taking advantage of the pretext (Captain Benyon happened to come into the consulate as he was starting, indulgently, to wait upon the ladies) to bring together "two parties" who, as he said, ought to appreciate each other, proposed to his fellow-officer in the service of the United States that he should go with him as witness of the little ceremony. He might, of course, take his clerk, but the captain would do much better; and he represented to Benyon that the Miss Theorys (singular name, wa' n't it?) suffered—he was sure—from a lack of society; also that one of them was very sick, that they were real pleasant and extraordinarily refined, and that the sight of a compatriot, literally draped, as it were, in the national banner, would cheer them up more than most anything, and give them a sense of protection. They had talked to the consul about Benyon's ship, which they could see from their windows, in the distance, at its anchorage. They were the only American ladies then at Naples,—the only residents, at least,—and the captain would n't be doing the polite thing unless he went to pay them his respects. Benyon felt afresh how little it was in his line to call upon strange women; he was not in the habit of hunting up female acquaintance, or of looking out for the soft emotions which the sex only can inspire. He had his reasons for this abstention, and he seldom relaxed it; but the consul appealed to him on rather strong grounds; and he suffered himself to be persuaded. He was far from regretting, during the first weeks at least, an act which was distinctly inconsistent with his great rule,—that of never exposing himself to the chance of seriously caring for an unmarried woman. He had been obliged to make this rule, and had adhered to it with some success. He was fond of women, but he was forced to restrict himself to superficial sentiments. There was no use tumbling into situations from which the only possible issue was a retreat The step he had taken with regard to poor Miss Theory and her delightful little sister was an exception on which at first he could only congratulate himself. That had been a happy idea of the ruminating old consul; it made Captain Benyon forgive him his hat, his boots, his shirtfront,—a costume which might be considered representative, and the effect of which was to make the observer turn with rapture to a half-naked lazzarone. On either side the acquaintance had helped the time to pass, and the hours he spent at the little *pension* at Posilippo left a sweet—and by no means innutritive—taste behind.

As the weeks went by his exception had grown to look a good deal like a rule; but he was able to remind himself that the path of retreat was always open to him. Moreover, if he should fall in love with the younger girl there would be no great harm, for Kate Theory was in love only with her sister, and it would matter very little to her whether he advanced or retreated. She was very attractive, or rather very attracting. Small, pale, attentive without rigidity, full of pretty curves and quick movements, she looked as if the habit of watching and serving had taken complete possession of her, and was literally a little sister of charity. Her thick black hair was pushed behind her ears, as if to help her to listen, and her clear brown eyes had the smile of a person too full of tact to cany a dull face to a sickbed. She spoke in an encouraging voice, and had soothing and unselfish habits. She was very pretty,—producing a cheerful effect of contrasted black and white, and dressed herself daintily, so that Mildred might have something agreeable to look at Benyon very soon perceived that there was a fund of good service in her. Her sister had it all now; but poor Miss Theory was fading fast, and then what would become of this precious little force? The answer to such a question that seemed most to the point was that it was none of his business. He was not sick,—at least not physically,—and he was not looking out for a nurse. Such a companion might be a luxury, but was not, as yet, a necessity: The welcome of the two ladies, at first, had been simple, and he scarcely knew what to call it but sweet; a bright, gentle friendliness remained the tone of their greeting. They evidently liked him to come,—they liked to see his big transatlantic ship hover about those gleaming coasts of exile. The fact of Miss Mildred being always stretched on her couch—in his successive visits to foreign waters Benyon had not unlearned (as why should he?) the pleasant American habit of using the lady's personal name—made their intimacy seem greater, their differences less; it was as if his hostesses had taken him into their confidence and he had been—as the consul would have said—of the same party. Knocking about the salt parts of the globe, with a few feet square on a rolling frigate for his only home, the pretty, flower-decked sitting-room of the quiet American sisters became, more than anything he had hitherto known, his interior. He had dreamed once of having an interior, but the dream had vanished in lurid smoke, and no such vision had come to him again. He had a feeling that the end of this was drawing nigh; he was sure that the advent of the strange brother, whose wife was certain to be disagreeable, would make a difference. That is why, as I have said, he came as often as possible the last week, after he had learned the day on which Percival Theory would arrive. The limits of the exception had been reached.

He had been new to the young ladies at Posilippo, and there was no reason why they should say to each other that he was a very different man from the ingenuous youth who, ten years before, used to wander with Georgina Gressie down vistas of plank fences brushed over with the advertisements of quack medicines. It was natural he should be, and we, who know him, would have found that he had traversed the whole scale of alteration. There was nothing ingenuous in him now; he had the look of experience, of having been seasoned and hardened by the years.

His face, his complexion, were the same; still smooth-shaven and slim, he always passed, at first, for a man scarcely out of his twenties. But his expression was old, and his talk was older still,—the talk of one who had seen much of the world (as indeed he had, to-day), and judged most things for himself, with a humorous scepticism which, whatever concessions it might make, superficially, for the sake of not offending (for instance) two remarkably nice American women, of the kind that had kept most of their illusions, left you with the conviction that the next minute it would go quickly back to its own standpoint There was a curious contradiction in him; he struck you as serious, and yet he could not be said to take things seriously. This was what made Kate Theory feel so sure that he had lost the object of his affections; and she said to herself that it must have been under circumstances of peculiar sadness, for that was, after all, a frequent accident, and was not usually thought, in itself, a sufficient stroke to make a man a cynic. This reflection, it may be added, was, on the young lady's part, just the least bit acrimonious. Captain Benyon was not a cynic in any sense in which he might have shocked an innocent mind; he kept his cynicism to himself, and was a very clever, courteous, attentive gentleman. If he was melancholy, you knew it chiefly by his jokes, for they were usually at his own expense; and if he was indifferent, it was all the more to his credit that he should have exerted himself to entertain his countrywomen.

The last time he called before the arrival of the expected brother, he found Miss Theory alone, and sitting up, for a wonder, at her window. Kate had driven into Naples to give orders at the hotel for the reception of the travellers, who required accommodation more spacious than the villa at Posilippo (where the two sisters had the best rooms) could offer them; and the sick girl had taken advantage of her absence and of the pretext afforded by a day of delicious warmth, to transfer herself, for the first time in six months, to an arm-chair. She was practising, as she said, for the long carriage-journey to the north, where, in a quiet corner they knew of, on the Lago Maggiore, her summer was to be spent. Eaymond Benyon remarked to her that she had evidently turned the corner and was going to get well, and this gave her a chance to say various things that were on her mind. She had many things on her mind, poor Mildred Theory, so caged and restless, and yet so resigned and patient as she was; with a clear, quick spirit, in the most perfect health, ever reaching forward, to the end of its tense little chain, from her wasted and suffering body; and, in the course of the perfect summer afternoon, as she sat there, exhilarated by the success of her effort to get up, and by her comfortable opportunity, she took her friendly visitor into the confidence of most of her anxieties. She told him, very promptly and positively, that she was not going to get well at all, that she had probably not more than ten months yet to live, and that he would oblige her very much by not forcing her to waste any more breath in contradicting him on that point. Of course she could n't talk much; therefore, she wished to say to him only things that he would not hear from any one else. Such, for instance, was her present secret—Katie's and hers—the secret of their fearing so much that they should n't like Percival's wife, who was not from Boston, but from New York. Naturally, that by itself would be nothing, but from what they had heard of her set—this subject had been explored by their correspondents—they were rather nervous, nervous to the point of not being in the least reassured by the fact that the young lady would bring Percival a fortune. The fortune was a matter of course, for that was just what they had heard about Agnes's circle—that the stamp of money was on all their thoughts and doings. They were very rich and very new and very splashing, and evidently had very little in common with the two Miss Theorys, who, moreover, if the truth must be told (and this was a great secret), did not care much for the letters their sister-in-law had hitherto addressed them. She had been at a French boarding-school in New York, and yet (and this was the greatest secret of all) she wrote to them that she had performed a part of the journey through France in *diligance!*

Of course, they would see the next day; Miss Mildred was sure she should know in a moment whether Agnes would like them. She could never have told him all this if her sister had been there, and Captain Benyon must promise never to reveal to Kate how she had chattered. Kate thought always that they must hide everything, and that even if Agnes should be a dreadful disappointment they must never let any one guess it And yet Kate was just the one who would suffer, in the coming years, after she herself had gone. Their brother had been everything to them, but now it would all be different Of course it was not to be expected that he should have remained a bachelor for their sake; she only wished he had waited till she was dead and Kate was married One of these events, it was true, was much less sure than the other; Kate might never marry,—much as she wished she would! She was quite morbidly unselfish, and did n't think she had a right to have anything of her own—not even a husband. Miss Mildred talked a good while about Kate, and it never occurred to her that she might bore Captain Benyon. She did n't, in point of fact; he had none of the trouble of wondering why this poor, sick, worried lady was trying to push her sister down his throat Their peculiar situation made everything natural, and the tone she took with him now seemed only what their pleasant relation for the last three months led up to. Moreover, he had an excellent reason for not being bored: the fact, namely, that after all, with regard to her sister, Miss Mildred appeared to him to keep back more than she uttered. She didn't tell him the great thing,— she had nothing to say as to what that charming girl thought of Eaymond Benyon. The effect of their interview, indeed, was to make him shrink from knowing, and he felt that the right thing for him would be to get back into his boat, which was waiting at the garden steps, before Kate Theory should return from Naples. It came over him, as he sat there, that he was far too interested in knowing what this young lady thought of him. She might think what she pleased; it could make no difference to him. The best opinion in the world—if it looked out at him from her tender eyes—would not make him a whit more free or more happy. Women of that sort were not for him, women whom one could not see familiarly without falling in love with them, and whom it was no use to fall in love with unless one was ready to marry them. The light of the summer afternoon, and of Miss Mildred's pure spirit, seemed suddenly to flood the whole subject. He saw that he was in danger, and he had long since made up his mind that from this particular peril it was not only necessary but honorable to flee. He took leave of his hostess before her sister reappeared, and had the courage even to say to her that he would not come back often after that; they would be so much occupied by their brother and his wife! As he moved across the glassy bay, to the rhythm of the oars, he wished either that the sisters would leave Naples or that his confounded commodore would send for him.

When Kate returned from her errand, ten minutes later, Milly told her of the captain's visit, and added that she had never seen anything so sudden as the way he left her. "He would n't wait for you, my dear, and he said he thought it more than likely that he should never see us again. It is as if he thought you were going to die too!"

"Is his ship called away?" Kate Theory asked.

"He did n't tell me so; he said we should be so busy with Percival and Agnes."

"He has got tired of us,—that's all. There's nothing wonderful in that; I knew he would."

Mildred said nothing for a moment; she was watching her sister, who was very attentively arranging some flowers. "Yes, of course, we are very dull, and he is like everybody else."

"I thought you thought he was so wonderful," said Kate, "and so fond of us."

"So he is; I am surer of that than ever. That's why he went away so abruptly."

Kate looked at her sister now. "I don't understand."

"Neither do I, darling. But you will, one of these days."

"How if he never comes back?"

"Oh, he will—after a while—when I am gone. Then he will explain; that, at least, is clear to me."

"My poor precious, as if I cared!" Kate Theory exclaimed, smiling as she distributed her flowers. She carried them to the window, to place them near her sister, and here she paused a moment, her eye caught by an object, far out in the bay, with which she was not unfamiliar. Mildred noticed its momentary look, and followed its direction.

"It's the captain's gig going back to the ship," Milly said. "It's so still one can almost hear the oars."

Kate Theory turned away, with a sudden, strange violence, a movement and exclamation which, the very next minute, as she became conscious of what she had said,—and, still more, of what she felt—smote her own heart (as it flushed her face) with surprise, and with the force of a revelation: "I wish it would sink him to the bottom of the sea!"

Her sister stared, then caught her by the dress, as she passed from her, drawing her back with a weak hand. "Oh, my dearest, my poorest!" And she pulled Kate down and down toward her, so that the girl had nothing for it but to sink on her knees and bury her face in Mildred's lap. If that ingenious invalid did not know everything now, she knew a great deal.

PART III.

V.

Mrs. Percival proved very pretty. It is more gracious to begin with this declaration, instead of saying that, in the first place, she proved very silly. It took a long day to arrive at the end of her silliness, and the two ladies at Posilippo, even after a week had passed, suspected that they had only skirted its edges. Kate Theory had not spent half an hour in her company before she gave a little private sigh of relief; she felt that a situation which had promised to be embarrassing was now quite clear, was even of a primitive simplicity. She would spend with her sister-in-law, in the coming time, one week in the year; that was all that was mortally possible. It was a blessing that one could see exactly what she was, for in that way the question settled itself. It would have been much more tiresome if Agnes had been a little less obvious; then she would have had to hesitate and consider and weigh one thing against another. She was pretty and silly, as distinctly as an orange is yellow and round; and Kate Theory would as soon have thought of looking to her to give interest to the future as she would have thought of looking to an orange to impart solidity to the prospect of dinner. Mrs. Percival travelled in the hope of meeting her American acquaintance, or of making acquaintance with such Americans as she did meet, and for the purpose of buying mementos for her relations. She was perpetually adding to her store of articles in tortoise-shell, in mother-of-pearl, in olive-wood, in ivory, in filigree, in tartan lacquer, in mosaic; and she had a collection of Roman scarfs and Venetian beads, which she looked over exhaustively every night before she went to bed. Her conversation bore mainly upon the manner in which she intended to dispose of these accumulations. She was constantly changing about, among each other, the persons to whom they were respectively to be offered. At Rome one of the first things she said to her husband after entering the Coliseum had been: "I guess I will give the ivory work-box to Bessie and the Roman pearls to

Aunt Harriet!" She was always hanging over the travellers' book at the hotel; she had it brought up to her, with a cup of chocolate, as soon as she arrived. She searched its pages for the magical name of New York, and she indulged in infinite conjecture as to who the people were—the name was sometimes only a partial cue—who had inscribed it there. What she most missed in Europe, and what she most enjoyed, were the New Yorkers; when she met them she talked about the people in their native city who had "moved" and the streets they had moved to. "Oh, yes, the Drapers are going up town, to Twenty-fourth Street, and the Vanderdeckens are going to be in Twenty-third Street, right back of them. My uncle, Henry Piatt, thinks of building round there." Mrs. Percival Theory was capable of repeating statements like these thirty times over,—of lingering on them for hours. She talked largely of herself, of her uncles and aunts, of her clothes—past, present, and future. These articles, in especial, filled her horizon; she considered them with a complacency which might have led you to suppose that she had invented the custom of draping the human form. Her main point of contact with Naples was the purchase of coral; and all the while she was there the word "set"—she used it as if every one would understand—fell with its little, flat, common sound upon the ears of her sisters-in-law, who had no sets of anything. She cared little for pictures and mountains; Alps and Apennines were not productive of New Yorkers, and it was difficult to take an interest in Madonnas who flourished at periods when, apparently, there were no fashions, or, at any rate, no trimmings.

I speak here not only of the impression she made upon her husband's anxious sisters, but of the judgment passed on her (he went so far as that, though it was not obvious how it mattered to him) by Raymond Benyon. And this brings me at a jump (I confess it's a very small one) to the fact that he did, after all, go back to Posilippo. He stayed away for nine days, and at the end of this time Percival Theory called upon him, to thank him for the civility he had shown his kinswomen. He went to this gentleman's hotel, to return his visit, and there he found Miss Kate, in her brother's sitting-room. She had come in by appointment from the villa, and was going with the others to seek the royal palace, which she had not yet had an opportunity to inspect It was proposed (not by Kate), and presently arranged, that Captain Benyon should go with them, and he accordingly walked over marble floors for half an hour, exchanging conscious commonplaces with the woman he loved. For this truth had rounded itself during those nine days of absence; he discovered that there was nothing particularly sweet in his life when once Kate Theory had been excluded from it He had stayed away to keep himself from falling in love with her; but this expedient was in itself illuminating, for he perceived that, according to the vulgar adage, he was locking the stable door after the horse had been stolen. As he paced the deck of his ship and looked toward Posilippo, his tenderness crystallized; the thick, smoky flame of a sentiment that knew itself forbidden and was angry at the knowledge, now danced upon the fuel of his good resolutions. The latter, it must be said, resisted, declined to be consumed. He determined that he would see Kate Theory again, for a time, just sufficient to bid her good-by, and to add a little explanation. He thought of his explanation very lovingly, but it may not strike the reader as a happy inspiration. To part from her dryly, abruptly, without an allusion to what he might have said if everything had been different,—that would be wisdom, of course, that would be virtue, that would be the line of a practical man, of a man who kept himself well in hand. But it would be virtue terribly unrewarded,—it would be virtue too austere for a person who sometimes flattered himself that he had taught himself stoicism. The minor luxury tempted him irresistibly, since the larger—that of happy love—was denied him; the luxury of letting the girl know that it would not be an accident—oh, not at all—that they should never meet again. She might easily think it was, and thinking it was would doubtless do her no harm. But this would n't give him his pleasure,—the Platonic satisfaction of expressing to her at the same time his belief that they might have made each other happy, and the necessity of his renunciation. That, probably, wouldn't hurt her either, for she had given him no proof whatever that she cared for him. The nearest approach to it was the way she walked beside him now, sweet and silent, without the least reference to his not having been back to the villa. The place was cool and dusky, the blinds were drawn, to keep out the light and noise, and the little party wandered through the high saloons, where precious marbles and the gleam of gilding and satin made reflections in the rich dimness. Here and there the cicerone, in slippers, with Neapolitan familiarity, threw open a shutter to show off a picture on a tapestry. He strolled in front with Percival

Theory and his wife, while this lady, drooping silently from her husband's arm as they passed, felt the stuff of the curtains and the sofas. When he caught her in these experiments, the cicerone, in expressive deprecation, clasped his hands and lifted his eyebrows; whereupon Mrs. Theory exclaimed to her husband, "Oh, bother his old king!" It was not striking to Captain Benyon why Percival Theory had married the niece of Mr. Henry Piatt. He was less interesting than his sisters,—a smooth, cool, correct young man, who frequently took out a pencil and did a little arithmetic on the back of a letter. He sometimes, in spite of his correctness, chewed a toothpick, and he missed the American papers, which he used to ask for in the most unlikely places. He was a Bostonian converted to New York; a very special type.

"Is it settled when you leave Naples?" Benyon asked of Kate Theory.

"I think so; on the twenty-fourth. My brother has been very kind; he has lent us his carriage, which is a large one, so that Mildred can lie down. He and Agnes will take another; but, of course, we shall travel together."

"I wish to Heaven I were going with you?" Captain Benyon said. He had given her the opportunity to respond, but she did not take it; she merely remarked, with a vague laugh, that of course he couldn't take his ship over the Apennines. "Yes, there is always my ship," he went on. "I am afraid that in future it will carry me far away from you."

They were alone in one of the royal apartments; their companions had passed, in advance of them, into the adjoining room. Benyon and his fellow-visitor had paused beneath one of the immense chandeliers of glass, which in the clear, colored gloom (through it one felt the strong outer light of Italy beating in) suspended its twinkling drops from the decorated vault. They looked round them confusedly, made shy for the moment by Benyon's having struck a note more serious than any that had hitherto souuded between them, looked at the sparse furniture, draped in white overalls, at the scagiiola floor, in which the great cluster of crystal pendants seemed to shine again.

"You are master of your ship. Can't you sail it as you like?" Kate Theory asked, with a smile.

"I am not master of anything. There is not a man in the world less free. I am a slave. I am a victim."

She looked at him with kind eyes; something in his voice suddenly made her put away all thought of the defensive airs that a girl, in certain situations, is expected to assume. She perceived that he wanted to make her understand something, and now her only wish was to help him to say it. "You are not happy," she murmured, simply, her voice dying away in a kind of wonderment at this reality.

The gentle touch of the words—it was as if her hand had stroked his cheek—seemed to him the sweetest thing he had ever known. "No, I am not happy, because I am not free. If I were—if I were, I would give up my ship. I would give up everything, to follow you. I can't explain; that is part of the hardness of it. I only want you to know it,—that if certain things were different, if everything was different, I might tell you that I believe I should have a right to speak to you. Perhaps some day it will change; but probably then it will be too late. Meanwhile, I have no right of any kind. I don't want to trouble you, and I don't ask of you—anything! It is only to have spoken just once. I don't make you understand, of course. I am afraid I seem to you rather a brute,—perhaps even a humbug. Don't think of it now,—don't try to understand. But some day, in the future, remember what I have said to you, and how we stood here, in this strange old place, alone! Perhaps it will give you a little pleasure."

Kate Theory began by listening to him with visible eagerness; but in a moment she turned away her eyes. "I am very sorry for you," she said, gravely.

"Then you do understand enough?"

"I shall think of what you have said, in the future."

Benyon's lips formed the beginning of a word of tenderness, which he instantly suppressed; and in a different tone, with a bitter smile and a sad shake of the head, raising his arms a moment and letting them fall, he said: "It won't hurt any one, your remembering this!"

"I don't know whom you mean." And the girl, abruptly, began to walk to the end of the room. He made no attempt to tell her whom he meant, and they proceeded together in silence till they overtook their companions.

There were several pictures in the neighboring room, and Percival Theory and his wife had stopped to look at one of them, of which the cicerone announced the title and the authorship as Benyon came up. It was a modern portrait of a Bourbon princess, a woman young, fair, handsome, covered with jewels. Mrs. Percival appeared to be more struck with it than with anything the palace had yet offered to her sight, while her sister-in-law walked to the window, which the custodian had opened, to look out into the garden. Benyon noticed this; he was conscious that he had given the girl something to reflect upon, and his ears burned a little as he stood beside Mrs. Percival and looked up, mechanically, at the royal lady. He already repented a little of what he had said, for, after all, what was the use? And he hoped the others wouldn't observe that he had been making love.

"Gracious, Percival! Do you see who she looks like?" Mrs. Theory said to her husband.

"She looks like a woman who has run up a big bill at Tiffany's," this gentleman answered.

"She looks like my sister-in-law; the eyes, the mouth, the way the hair's done,—the whole thing."

"Which do you mean? You have got about a dozen."

"Why, Georgina, of course,—Georgina Roy. She's awfully like."

"Do you call *her* your sister-in-law?" Percival Theory asked. "You must want very much to claim her."

"Well, she's handsome enough. You have got to invent some new name, then. Captain Benyon, what do you call your brother-in-law's second wife?" Mrs. Percival continued, turning to her neighbor, who still stood staring at the portrait. At first he had looked without seeing; then sight, and hearing as well, became quick. They were suddenly peopled with thrilling recognitions.

The Bourbon princess—the eyes, the mouth, the way the hair was done; these things took on an identity, and the gaze of the painted face seemed to fasten itself to his own. But who in the world was Georgina Roy, and what was this talk about sisters-in-law? He turned to the little lady at his side a countenance unexpectedly puzzled by the problem she had airily presented to him.

"Your brother-in-law's second wife? That's rather complicated."

"Well, of course, he need n't have married again?" said Mrs. Percival, with a small sigh.

"Whom did he marry?" asked Benyon, staring.

Percival Theory had turned away. "Oh, if you are going into her relationships!" he murmured, and joined his sister at the brilliant window, through which, from the distance, the many-voiced uproar of Naples came in.

"He married first my sister Dora, and she died five years ago. Then he married *her*," and Mrs. Percival nodded at the princess.

Benyon's eyes went back to the portrait; he could see what she meant—it stared out at him. "Her? Georgina?"

"Georgina Gressie. Gracious, do you know her?"

It was very distinct—that answer of Mrs. Percival's, and the question that followed it as well. But he had the resource of the picture; he could look at it, seem to take it very seriously, though it danced up and down before him. He felt that he was turning red, then he felt that he was turning pale. "The brazen impudence!" That was the way he could speak to himself now of the woman he had once loved, and whom he afterwards hated, till this had died out, too. Then the wonder of it was lost in the quickly growing sense that it would make a difference for him,—a great difference. Exactly what, he didn't see yet; only a difference that swelled and swelled as he thought of it, and caught up, in its expansion, the girl who stood behind him so quietly, looking into the Italian garden.

The custodian drew Mrs. Percival away to show her another princess, before Benyon answered her last inquiry. This gave him time to recover from his first impulse, which had been to answer it with a negative; he saw in a moment that an admission of his acquaintance with Mrs. Roy (Mrs. Roy!—it was prodigious!) was necessarily helping him to learn more. Besides, it needn't be compromising. Very likely Mrs. Percival would hear one day that he had once wanted to marry her. So, when he joined his companions a minute later he remarked that he had known Miss Gressie years before, and had even admired her considerably, but had lost sight of her entirely in later days. She had been a great beauty, and it was a wonder that she had not married earlier. Five years ago, was it? No, it was only two. He had been going to say that in so long a time it would have been singular he should not have heard of it. He had been away from New York for ages; but one always heard of marriages and deaths. This was a proof, though two years was rather long. He led Mrs. Percival insidiously into a further room, in advance of the others, to whom the cicerone returned. She was delighted to talk about her "connections," and she supplied him with every detail He could trust himself now; his self-possession was complete, or, so far as it was wanting, the fault was that of a sudden gayety which he could not, on the spot, have accounted for. Of course it was not very flattering to them—Mrs. Percivals own people—that poor Dora's husband should have consoled himself; but men always did it (talk of widows!) and he had chosen a girl who was—well, very fine-looking, and the sort of successor to Dora that they needn't be ashamed of. She had been awfully admired, and no one had understood why she had waited so long to marry. She had had some affair as a girl,—an engagement to an officer in the army,—and the man had jilted her, or they had quarrelled, or something or other. She was almost an old maid,—well, she was thirty, or very nearly,—but she had done something good now. She was handsomer than ever, and tremendously stylish. William Roy had one of the biggest incomes in the city, and he was quite affectionate. He had been intensely fond of Dora—he often spoke of her still, at least to her own relations; and her portrait, the last time Mrs. Percival was in his house (it was at a party, after his marriage to Miss Gressie), was still in the front parlor.. Perhaps by this time he had had it moved to the back; but she was sure he would keep it somewhere, anyway.

Poor Dora had had no children; but Georgina was making that all right,—
she had a beautiful boy. Mrs. Percival had what she would have called quite
a pleasant chat with Captain Benyon about Mrs. Roy. Perhaps *he* was the
officer—she never thought of that? He was sure he had never jilted her? And
he had never quarrelled with a lady? Well, he must be different from most
men.

He certainly had the air of being so, before he parted that afternoon
with Kate Theory. This young lady, at least, was free to think him wanting
in that consistency which is supposed to be a distinctively masculine virtue.
An hour before, he had taken an eternal farewell of her, and now he was
alluding to future meetings, to future visits, proposing that, with her sister-
in-law, she should appoint an early day for coming to see the "Louisiana."
She had supposed she understood him, but it would appear now that she
had not understood him at all. His manner had changed, too. More and
more off his guard, Raymond Benyon was not aware how much more hopeful
an expression it gave him, his irresistible sense that somehow or other this
extraordinary proceeding of his wife's would set him free. Kate Theory felt
rather weary and mystified,—all the more for knowing that henceforth
Captain Benyon's variations would be the most important thing in life for
her.

This officer, on his ship in the bay, lingered very late on deck that
night,—lingered there, indeed, under the warm southern sky, in which the
stars glittered with a hot, red light, until the early dawn began to show. He
smoked cigar after cigar, he walked up and down by the hour, he was agitated
by a thousand reflections, he repeated to himself that it made a difference,—
an immense difference; but the pink light had deepened in the east before
he had discovered in what the diversity consisted. By that time he saw it
clearly,—it consisted in Georgina's being in his power now, in place of his
being in hers. He laughed as he sat there alone in the darkness at the thought
of what she had done. It had occurred to him more than once that she would
do it,—he believed her capable of anything; but the accomplished fact had a
freshness of comicality. He thought of Mr. William Roy, of his big income,
of his being "quite affectionate," of his blooming son and heir, of his having

found such a worthy successor to poor Mrs. Dora. He wondered whether Georgina had happened to mention to him that she had a husband living, but was strongly of the belief that she had not. Why should she, after all? She had neglected to mention it to so many others. He had thought he knew her, in so many years,—that he had nothing more to learn about her; but this ripe stroke revived his sense of her audacity. Of course it was what she had been waiting for, and if she had not done it sooner it was because she had hoped he would be lost at sea in one of his long cruises and relieve her of the necessity of a crime. How she must hate him to-day for not having been lost, for being alive, for continuing to put her in the wrong! Much as she hated him, however, his own loathing was at least a match for hers. She had done him the foulest of wrongs,—she had ravaged his life. That he should ever detest in this degree a woman whom he had once loved as he loved her, he would not have thought possible in his innocent younger years. But he would not have thought it possible then that a woman should be such a cold-blooded devil as she had been. His love had perished in his rage,—his blinding, impotent rage at finding that he had been duped, and measuring his impotence. When he learned, years before, from Mrs. Portico, what she had done with her baby, of whose entrance into life she herself had given him no intimation, he felt that he was face to face with a full revelation of her nature. Before that it had puzzled him; it had amazed him; his relations with her were bewildering, stupefying. But when, after obtaining, with difficulty and delay, a leave of absence from Government, and betaking himself to Italy to look for the child and assume possession of it, he had encountered absolute failure and defeat,—then the case presented itself to him more simply. He perceived that he had mated himself with a creature who just happened to be a monster, a human exception altogether. That was what he could n't pardon—her conduct about the child; never, never, never! To him she might have done what she chose,—dropped him, pushed him out into eternal cold, with his hands fast tied,—and he would have accepted it, excused her almost, admitted that it had been his business to mind better what he was about. But she had tortured him through the poor little irrecoverable son whom he had never seen, through the heart and the vitals that she had not herself, and that he had to have, poor wretch, for both of them!

63

All his efforts for years had been to forget these horrible months, and he had cut himself off from them so that they seemed at times to belong to the life of another person. But to-night he lived them over again; he retraced the different gradations of darkness through which he had passed, from the moment, so soon after his extraordinary marriage, when it came over him that she already repented, and meant, if possible, to elude all her obligations. This was the moment when he saw why she had reserved herself—in the strange vow she extracted from him—an open door for retreat; the moment, too, when her having had such an inspiration (in the midst of her momentary good faith, if good faith it had ever been) struck him as a proof of her essential depravity. What he had tried to forget came back to him: the child that was not his child produced for him when he fell upon that squalid nest of peasants in the Genoese country; and then the confessions, retractations, contradictions, lies, terrors, threats, and general bottomless, baffling baseness of every one in the place. The child was gone; that had been the only definite thing. The woman who had taken it to nurse had a dozen different stories,—her husband had as many,—and every one in the village had a hundred more. Georgina had been sending money,—she had managed, apparently, to send a good deal,—and the whole country seemed to have been living on it and making merry. At one moment the baby had died and received a most expensive burial; at another he had been intrusted (for more healthy air, Santissima Madonna!) to the woman's cousin in another village. According to a version, which for a day or two Benyon had inclined to think the least false, he had been taken by the cousin (for his beauty's sake) to Genoa (when she went for the first time in her life to the town to see her daughter in service there), and had been confided for a few hours to a third woman, who was to keep him while the cousin walked about the streets, but who, having no child of her own, took such a fancy to him that she refused to give him up, and a few days later left the place (she was a Pisana) never to be heard of more. The cousin had forgotten her name,—it had happened six months before. Benyon spent a year looking up and down Italy for his child, and inspecting hundreds of swaddled infants, impenetrable candidates for recognition. Of course he could only get further and further from real knowledge, and his search was arrested by the conviction that it was making him mad. He set his teeth and made up his mind (or tried to) that the baby had died in the hands of its nurse. This was, after all, much the likeliest supposition, and the woman had maintained it, in the hope of being rewarded for her candor, quite as often as she had asseverated that it was still, somewhere, alive, in the hope of being remunerated for her good news. It may be imagined with what sentiments toward his wife Benyon had emerged from this episode. To-night his memory went further back,—back to the beginning and to the days when he had had to ask himself, with all the crudity of his first surprise, what in the name of wantonness she had wished to do with him. The answer to this speculation was so old,—it had dropped so ont of the line of recurrence,— that it was now almost new again. Moreover, it was only approximate, for, as I have already said, he could comprehend such conduct as little at the end as at the beginning. She had found herself on a slope which her nature forced her to descend to the bottom. She did him the honor of wishing to enjoy his society, and she did herself the honor of thinking that their intimacy— however brief—must have a certain consecration. She felt that, with him, after his promise (he would have made any promise to lead her on), she was secure,—secure as she had proved to be, secure as she must think herself now. That security had helped her to ask herself, after the first flush of passion was over, and her native, her twice-inherited worldliness had bad time to open its eyes again, why she should keep faith with a man whose deficiencies (as a husband before the world—another affair) had been so scientifically exposed to her by her parents. So she had simply determined not to keep faith; and her determination, at least, she did keep.

By the time Benyon turned in he had satisfied himself, as I say, that Georgina was now in his power; and this seemed to him such an improvement in his situation that he allowed himself (for the next ten days) a license which made Kate Theory almost as happy as it made her sister, though she pretended to understand it far less. Mildred sank to her rest, or rose to fuller comprehensions, within the year, in the Isle of Wight, and Captain Benyon, who had never written so many letters as since they left Naples, sailed westward about the same time as the sweet survivor. For the "Louisiana" at last was ordered home.

VI.

Certainly, I will see you if you come, and you may appoint any day or hour you like. I should have seen you with pleasure any time these last years. Why should we not be friends, as we used to be? Perhaps we shall be yet. I say "perhaps" only, on purpose,—because your note is rather vague about your state of mind. Don't come with any idea about making me nervous or uncomfortable. I am not nervous by nature, thank Heaven, and I won't—I positively won't (do you hear, dear Captain Benyon?)—be uncomfortable. I have been so (it served me right) for years and years; but I am very happy now. To remain so is the very definite intention of, yours ever,

Georgina Roy.

This was the answer Benyon received to a short letter that he despatched to Mrs. Roy after his return to America. It was not till he had been there some weeks that he wrote to her. He had been occupied in various ways: he had had to look after his ship; he had had to report at Washington; he had spent a fortnight with his mother at Portsmouth, N. H.; and he had paid a visit to Kate Theory in Boston. She herself was paying visits, she was staying with various relatives and friends. She had more color—it was very delicately rosy—than she had had of old, in spite of her black dress; and the effect of looking at him seemed to him to make her eyes grow still prettier. Though sisterless now, she was not without duties, and Benyon could easily see that life would press hard on her unless some one should interfere. Every one regarded her as just the person to do certain things. Every one thought she could do everything, because she had nothing else to do. She used to read to the blind, and, more onerously, to the deaf. She looked after other people's children while the parents attended anti-slavery conventions.

She was coming to New York later to spend a week at her brother's, but beyond this she didn't know what she should do. Benyon felt it to be awkward that he should not be able, just now, to tell her; and this had much to do with his coming to the point, for he accused himself of having rather hung fire. Coming to the point, for Benyon, meant writing a note to Mrs. Roy (as he must call her), in which he asked whether she would see him if he should present himself. The missive was short; it contained, in addition to what I have noted, little more than the remark that he had something of importance to say to her. Her reply, which we have just read, was prompt. Benyon designated an hour, and the next day rang the doorbell of her big modern house, whose polished windows seemed to shine defiance at him.

As he stood on the steps, looking up and down the straight vista of the Fifth Avenue, he perceived that he was trembling a little, that *he* was nervous, if she was not. He was ashamed of his agitation, and he addressed himself a very stern reprimand. Afterwards he saw that what had made him nervous was not any doubt of the goodness of his cause, but his revived sense (as he drew near her) of his wife's hardness,—her capacity for insolence. He might only break himself against that, and the prospect made him feel helpless. She kept him waiting for a long time after he had been introduced; and as he walked up and down her drawing-room, an immense, florid, expensive apartment, covered with blue satin, gilding, mirrors and bad frescos, it came over him as a certainty that her delay was calculated. She wished to annoy him, to weary him; she was as ungenerous as she was unscrupulous. It never occurred to him that in spite of the bold words of her note, she, too, might be in a tremor, and if any one in their secret had suggested that she was afraid to meet him, he would have laughed at this idea. This was of bad omen for the success of his errand; for it showed that he recognized the ground of her presumption,—his having the superstition of old promises. By the time she appeared, he was flushed,—very angry. She closed the door behind her, and stood there looking at him, with the width of the room between them.

The first emotion her presence excited was a quick sense of the strange fact that, after all these years of loneliness, such a magnificent person should be his wife. For she was magnificent, in the maturity of her beauty, her head erect, her complexion splendid, her auburn tresses undimmed, a certain plenitude in her very glance. He saw in a moment that she wished to seem to him beautiful, she had endeavored to dress herself to the best effect. Perhaps, after all, it was only for this she had delayed; she wished to give herself every possible touch. For some moments they said nothing; they had not stood face to face for nearly ten years, and they met now as adversaries. No two persons could possibly be more interested in taking each other's measure. It scarcely belonged to Georgina, however, to have too much the air of timidity; and after a moment, satisfied, apparently, that she was not to receive a broadside, she advanced, slowly rubbing her jewelled hands and smiling. He wondered why she should smile, what thought was in her mind. His impressions followed each other with extraordinary quickness of pulse, and now he saw, in addition to what he had already perceived, that she was waiting to take her cue,—she had determined on no definite line. There was nothing definite about her but her courage; the rest would depend upon him. As for her courage, it seemed to glow in the beauty which grew greater as she came nearer, with her eyes on his and her fixed smile; to be expressed in the very perfume that accompanied her steps. By this time he had got still a further impression, and it was the strangest of all. She was ready for anything, she was capable of anything, she wished to surprise him with her beauty, to remind him that it belonged, after all, at the bottom of everything, to him. She was ready to bribe him, if bribing should be necessary. She had carried on an intrigue before she was twenty; it would be more, rather than less, easy for her, now that she was thirty. All this and more was in her cold, living eyes, as in the prolonged silence they engaged themselves with his; but I must not dwell upon it, for reasons extraneous to the remarkable fact She was a truly amazing creature.

"Raymond!" she said, in a low voice, a voice which might represent either a vague greeting or an appeal.

He took no heed of the exclamation, but asked her why she had deliberately kept him waiting,—as if she had not made a fool enough of him already. She could n't suppose it was for his pleasure he had come into the house.

She hesitated a moment,—still with her smile. "I must tell you I have a son,—the dearest little boy. His nurse happened to be engaged for the moment, and I had to watch him. I am more devoted to him than you might suppose."

He fell back from her a few steps. "I wonder if you are insane," he murmured.

"To allude to my child? Why do you ask me such questions then? I tell you the simple truth. I take every care of this one. I am older and wiser. The other one was a complete mistake; he had no right to exist."

"Why didn't you kill him then with your own hands, instead of that torture?"

"Why did n't I kill myself? That question would be more to the point You are looking wonderfully well," she broke off in another tone; "had n't we better sit down?"

"I did n't come here for the advantage of conversation," Benyon answered. And he was going on, but she interrupted him—

"You came to say something dreadful, very likely; though I hoped you would see it was better not But just tell me this before you begin. Are you successful, are you happy? It has been so provoking, not knowing more about you."

There was something in the manner in which this was said that caused him to break into a loud laugh; whereupon she added,—

"Your laugh is just what it used to be. How it comes back to me! You *have* improved in appearance," she went on.

She had seated herself, though he remained standing; and she leaned back in a low, deep chair, looking up at him, with her arms folded. He stood near her and over her, as it were, dropping his baffled eyes on her, with his hand resting on the corner of the chimney-piece. "Has it never occurred to you that I may deem myself absolved from the promise made you before I married you?"

"Very often, of course. But I have instantly dismissed the idea. How can you be 'absolved'? One promises, or one doesn't. I attach no meaning to that, and neither do you." And she glanced down to the front of her dress.

Benyon listened, but he went on as if he had not heard her. "What I came to say to you is this: that I should like your consent to my bringing a suit for divorce against you."

"A suit for divorce? I never thought of that."

"So that I may marry another woman. I can easily obtain a divorce on the ground of your desertion."

She stared a moment, then her smile solidified, as it were, and she looked grave; but he could see that her gravity, with her lifted eyebrows, was partly assumed. "Ah, you want to marry another woman!" she exclaimed, slowly, thoughtfully. He said nothing, and she went on: "Why don't you do as I have done?"

"Because I don't want my children to be—"

Before he could say the words she sprang up, checking him with a cry. "Don't say it; it is n't necessary! Of course I know what you mean; but they won't be if no one knows it."

"I should object to knowing it myself; it's enough for me to know it of yours."

"Of course I have been prepared for your saying that"

"I should hope so!" Benyon exclaimed. "You may be a bigamist if it suits you, but to me the idea is not attractive. I wish to marry—" and, hesitating a moment, with his slight stammer, he repeated, "I wish to marry—"

"Marry, then, and have done with it!" cried Mrs. Roy.

He could already see that he should be able to extract no consent from her; he felt rather sick. "It's extraordinary to me that you should n't be more afraid of being found out," he said after a moment's reflection. "There are two or three possible accidents."

"How do you know how much afraid I am? I have thought of every accident, in dreadful nights. How do you know what my life is, or what it has been all these miserable years?"

"You look wasted and worn, certainly."

"Ah, don't compliment me!" Georgina exclaimed. "If I had never known you—if I had not been through all this—I believe I should have been handsome. When did you hear of my marriage? Where were you at the time?"

"At Naples, more than six months ago, by a mere chance."

"How strange that it should have taken you so long! Is the lady a Neapolitan? They don't mind what they do over there."

"I have no information to give you beyond what I just said," Benyon rejoined. "My life does n't in the least regard you."

"Ah, but it does from the moment I refuse to let you divorce me."

"You refuse?" Benyon said softly.

"Don't look at me that way! You have n't advanced so rapidly as I used to think you would; you haven't distinguished yourself so much," she went on, irrelevantly.

"I shall be promoted commodore one of these days," Benyon answered. "You don't know much about it, for my advancement has already been very exceptionally rapid." He blushed as soon as the words were out of his mouth. She gave a light laugh on seeing it; but he took up his hat and added: "Think over a day or two what I have proposed to you. Think of the temper in which I ask it."

"The temper?" she stared. "Pray, what have you to do with temper?" And as he made no reply, smoothing his hat with his glove, she went on: "Years ago, as much as you please I you had a good right, I don't deny, and you raved, in your letters, to your heart's content That's why I would n't see you; I did n't wish to take it full in the face. But that's all over now, time is a healer, you have cooled off, and by your own admission you have consoled yourself. Why do you talk to me about temper! What in the world have I done to you, but let you alone?"

"What do you call this business?" Benyon asked, with his eye flashing all over the room.

"Ah, excuse me, that doesn't touch you,—it's my affair. I leave you your liberty, and I can live as I like. If I choose to live in this way, it may be queer (I admit it is, awfully), but you have nothing to say to it. If I am willing to take the risk, you may be. If I am willing to play such an infernal trick upon a confiding gentleman (I will put it as strongly as you possibly could), I don't see what you have to say to it except that you are tremendously glad such a woman as that is n't known to be your wife!" She had been cool and deliberate up to this time; but with these words her latent agitation broke out "Do you think I have been happy? Do you think I have enjoyed existence? Do you see me freezing up into a stark old maid?"

"I wonder you stood out so long!" said Benyon.

"I wonder I did. They were bad years."

"I have no doubt they were!"

"You could do as you pleased," Georgina went on. "You roamed about the world; you formed charming relations. I am delighted to hear it from your own lips. Think of my going back to my father's house—that family vault—and living there, year after year, as Miss Gressie! If you remember my father and mother—they are round in Twelfth Street, just the same—you must admit that I paid for my folly!"

"I have never understood you; I don't understand you now," said Benyon.

She looked at him a moment. "I adored you."

"I could damn you with a word!" he went on.

The moment he had spoken she grasped his arm and held up her other hand, as if she were listening to a sound outside the room. She had evidently had an inspiration, and she carried it into instant effect She swept away to the door, flung it open, and passed into the hall, whence her voice came back to Benyon as she addressed a person who was apparently her husband. She had heard him enter the house at his habitual hour, after his long morning at business; the closing of the door of the vestibule had struck her ear. The parlor was on a level with the hall, and she greeted him without impediment.

She asked him to come in and be introduced to Captain Benyon, and he responded with due solemnity. She returned in advance of him, her eyes fixed upon Benyon and lighted with defiance, her whole face saying to him, vividly: "Here is your opportunity; I give it to you with my own hands. Break your promise and betray me if you dare! You say you can damn me with a word: speak the word and let us see!"

Benyon's heart beat faster, as he felt that it was indeed a chance; but half his emotion came from the spectacle—magnificent in its way—of her unparalleled impudence. A sense of all that he had escaped in not having had to live with her rolled over him like a wave, while he looked strangely at Mr. Roy, to whom this privilege had been vouchsafed. He saw in a moment his successor had a constitution that would carry it. Mr. Roy suggested squareness and solidity; he was a broadbased, comfortable, polished man, with a surface in which the rank tendrils of irritation would not easily obtain a foothold. He had a broad, blank face, a capacious mouth, and a small, light eye, to which, as he entered, he was engaged in adjusting a double gold-rimmed glass. He approached Benyon with a prudent, civil, punctual air, as if he habitually met a good many gentlemen in the course of business, and though, naturally, this was not that sort of occasion he was not a man to waste time in preliminaries. Benyon had immediately the impression of having seen him—or his equivalent—a thousand times before. He was middle-aged, fresh-colored, whiskered, prosperous, indefinite. Georgina introduced them to each other. She spoke of Benyon as an old friend whom she had known long before she had known Mr. Roy, who had been very kind to her years ago, when she was a girl.

"He's in the navy. He has just come back from a long cruise."

Mr. Hoy shook hands,—Benyon gave him his before he knew it,—said he was very happy, smiled, looked at Benyon from head to foot, then at Georgina, then round the room, then back at Benyon again,—at Benyon, who stood there, without sound or movement, with a dilated eye, and a pulse quickened to a degree of which Mr. Roy could have little idea. Georgina made some remark about their sitting down, but William Roy replied that he had n't time for that,—if Captain Benyon would excuse him. He should have to go straight into the library, and write a note to send back to his office, where, as he just remembered, he had neglected to give, in leaving the place, an important direction.

"You can wait a moment, surely," Georgina said. "Captain Benyon wants so much to see you."

"Oh, yes, my dear; I can wait a minute, and I can come back."

Benyon saw, accordingly, that he was waiting, and that Georgina was waiting too. Each was waiting for him to say something, though they were waiting for different things. Mr. Roy put his hands behind him, balanced himself on his toes, hoped that Captain Benyon had enjoyed his cruise,— though he should n't care much for the navy himself,—and evidently wondered at the stolidity of his wife's visitor. Benyon knew he was speaking, for he indulged in two or three more observations, after which he stopped. But his meaning was not present to our hero. This personage was conscious of only one thing, of his own momentary power,—of everything that hung on his lips; all the rest swam before him; there was vagueness in his ears and eyes. Mr. Roy stopped, as I say, and there was a pause, which seemed to Benyon of tremendous length. He knew, while it lasted, that Georgina was as conscious as himself that he felt his opportunity, that he held it there in his hand, weighing it noiselessly in the palm, and that she braved and scorned, or, rather, that she enjoyed, the danger. He asked himself whether he should be able to speak if he were to try, and then he knew that he should not, that the words would stick in his throat, that he should make sounds that would dishonor his cause. There was no real choice or decision, then, on Benyon's part; his silence was after all the same old silence, the fruit of other hours and places, the stillness to which Georgina listened, while he felt her eager eyes fairly eat into his face, so that his cheeks burned with the touch of them. The moments stood before him in their turn; each one was distinct. "Ah, well," said Mr. Roy, "perhaps I interrupt,—I 'll just dash off my note" Benyon knew that he was rather bewildered, that he was making a pretext, that he was leaving the room; knew presently that Georgina again stood before him alone.

"You are exactly the man I thought you!" she announced, as joyously as if she had won a bet.

"You are the most horrible woman I can imagine. Good God! if I *had* had to live with you!" That is what he said to her in answer.

Even at this she never flushed; she continued to smile in triumph. "He adores me—but what's that to you? Of course you have all the future," she went on; "but I know you as if I had made you!"

Benyon reflected a moment "If he adores you, you are all right. If our divorce is pronounced, you will be free, and then he can marry you properly, which he would like ever so much better."

"It's too touching to hear you reason about it. Fancy me telling such a hideous story—about myself—me—*me*!" And she touched her breasts with her white fingers.

Benyon gave her a look that was charged with all the sickness of his helpless rage. "You—*you*!" he repeated, as he turned away from her and passed through the door which Mr. Roy had left open.

She followed him into the hall, she was close behind him; he moved before her as she pressed. "There was one more reason," she said. "I would n't be forbidden. It was my hideous pride. That's what prevents me now."

"I don't care what it is," Benyon answered, wearily, with his hand on the knob of the door.

She laid hers on his shoulder; he stood there an instant feeling it, wishing that her loathsome touch gave him the right to strike her to the earth,—to strike her so that she should never rise again.

"How clever you are, and intelligent always,—as you used to be; to feel so perfectly and know so well, without more scenes, that it's hopeless—my ever consenting! If I have, with you, the shame of having made you promise, let me at least have the profit!"

His back had been turned to her, but at this he glanced round. "To hear you talk of shame—!"

"You don't know what I have gone through; but, of course, I don't ask any pity from you. Only I should like to say something kind to you before we part I admire you, esteem you: I don't many people! Who will ever tell her, if you don't? How will she ever know, then? She will be as safe as I am. You know what that is," said Georgina, smiling.

He had opened the door while she spoke, apparently not heeding her, thinking only of getting away from her forever. In reality he heard every word she said, and felt to his marrow the lowered, suggestive tone in which she made him that last recommendation. Outside, on the steps—she stood there in the doorway—he gave her his last look. "I only hope you will die. I shall pray for that!" And he descended into the street and took his way.

It was after this that his real temptation came. Not the temptation to return betrayal for betrayal; that passed away even in a few days, for he simply knew that he couldn't break his promise, that it imposed itself on him as stubbornly as the color of his eyes or the stammer of his lips; it had gone forth into the world to live for itself, and was far beyond his reach or his authority. But the temptation to go through the form of a marriage with Kate Theory, to let her suppose that he was as free as herself, and that their children, if they should have any, would, before the law, have a right to exist,—this attractive idea held him fast for many weeks, and caused him to pass some haggard nights and days. It was perfectly possible she might learn his secret, and that, as no one could either suspect it or have an interest in bringing it to light, they both might live and die in security and honor. This vision fascinated him; it was, I say, a real temptation. He thought of other solutions,—of telling her that he was married (without telling her to whom), and inducing her to overlook such an accident, and content herself with a ceremony in which the world would see no flaw. But after all the contortions of his spirit it remained as clear to him as before that dishonor was in everything but renunciation. So, at last, he renounced. He took two steps which attested ths act to himself. He addressed an urgent request to the Secretary of the Navy that he might, with as little delay as possible, be despatched on another long voyage; and he returned to Boston to tell Kate Theory that they must wait. He could explain so little that, say what he would, he was aware that he could not make his conduct seem natural, and he saw that the girl only trusted him,—that she never understood. She trusted without understanding, and she agreed to wait. When the writer of these pages last heard of the pair they were waiting still.

GLASSES

CHAPTER I

Yes indeed, I say to myself, pen in hand, I can keep hold of the thread and let it lead me back to the first impression. The little story is all there, I can touch it from point to point; for the thread, as I call it, is a row of coloured beads on a string. None of the beads are missing—at least I think they're not: that's exactly what I shall amuse myself with finding out.

I had been all summer working hard in town and then had gone down to Folkestone for a blow. Art was long, I felt, and my holiday short; my mother was settled at Folkestone, and I paid her a visit when I could. I remember how on this occasion, after weeks in my stuffy studio with my nose on my palette, I sniffed up the clean salt air and cooled my eyes with the purple sea. The place was full of lodgings, and the lodgings were at that season full of people, people who had nothing to do but to stare at one another on the great flat down. There were thousands of little chairs and almost as many little Jews; and there was music in an open rotunda, over which the little Jews wagged their big noses. We all strolled to and fro and took pennyworths of rest; the long, level cliff-top, edged in places with its iron rail, might have been the deck of a huge crowded ship. There were old folks in Bath chairs, and there was one dear chair, creeping to its last full stop, by the side of which I always walked. There was in fine weather the coast of France to look at, and there were the usual things to say about it; there was also in every state of the atmosphere our friend Mrs. Meldrum, a subject of remark not less inveterate. The widow of an officer in the Engineers, she had settled, like many members of the martial miscellany, well within sight of the hereditary enemy, who however had left her leisure to form in spite of the difference of their years a close alliance with my mother. She was the heartiest, the keenest, the ugliest of women, the least apologetic, the least morbid in her misfortune. She carried it high aloft with loud sounds and free gestures, made it flutter in the breeze as if it had been the flag of her country. It consisted mainly of a big red face, indescribably out of drawing, from which she glared at you through gold-rimmed aids to vision, optic circles of such diameter and so frequently displaced that some one had vividly spoken of her as flattering her nose against the glass of her spectacles. She was extraordinarily near-sighted, and whatever they did to other objects they magnified immensely the kind eyes behind them. Blest conveniences they were, in their hideous, honest strength—they showed the good lady everything in the world but her own queerness. This element was enhanced by wild braveries of dress, reckless charges of colour and stubborn resistances of cut, wondrous encounters in which the art of the toilet seemed to lay down its life. She had the tread of a grenadier and the voice of an angel.

In the course of a walk with her the day after my arrival I found myself grabbing her arm with sudden and undue familiarity. I had been struck by the beauty of a face that approached us and I was still more affected when I saw the face, at the sight of my companion, open like a window thrown wide. A smile fluttered out of it an brightly as a drapery dropped from a sill—a drapery shaken there in the sun by a young lady flanked by two young men, a wonderful young lady who, as we drew nearer, rushed up to Mrs. Meldrum with arms flourished for an embrace. My immediate impression of her had been that she was dressed in mourning, but during the few moments she stood talking with our friend I made more discoveries. The figure from the neck down was meagre, the stature insignificant, but the desire to please towered high, as well as the air of infallibly knowing how and of never, never missing it. This was a little person whom I would have made a high bid for a good chance to paint. The head, the features, the colour, the whole facial oval and radiance had a wonderful purity; the deep grey eyes—the most agreeable, I thought, that I had ever seen—brushed with a kind of winglike grace every object they encountered. Their possessor was just back from Boulogne, where she had spent a week with dear Mrs. Floyd-Taylor: this accounted for the effusiveness of her reunion with dear Mrs. Meldrum. Her black garments were of the freshest and daintiest; she suggested a pink-and-white wreath at a showy funeral. She confounded us for three minutes with her presence; she was a beauty of the great conscious public responsible order. The young men, her companions, gazed at her and grinned: I could see there were very few moments of the day at which young men, these or others, would not be so occupied. The people who approached took leave of their manners; every one seemed to linger and gape. When she brought her face close to Mrs. Meldrum's—and she appeared to be always bringing it close to somebody's—it was a marvel that objects so dissimilar should express the same general identity, the unmistakable character of the English gentlewoman. Mrs. Meldrum sustained the comparison with her usual courage, but I wondered why she didn't introduce me: I should have had no objection to the bringing of such a face close to mine. However, by the time the young lady moved on with her escort she herself bequeathed me a sense that some such *rapprochement* might still occur. Was this by reason of the general frequency of encounters at Folkestone, or by reason of a subtle acknowledgment that she contrived to make of the rights, on the part of others, that such beauty as hers created? I was in a position to answer that question after Mrs. Meldrum had answered a few of mine.

CHAPTER II

Flora Saunt, the only daughter of an old soldier, had lost both her parents, her mother within a few months. Mrs. Meldrum had known them, disapproved of them, considerably avoided them: she had watched the girl, off and on, from her early childhood. Flora, just twenty, was extraordinarily alone in the world—so alone that she had no natural chaperon, no one to stay with but a mercenary stranger, Mrs. Hammond Synge, the sister-in-law of one of the young men I had just seen. She had lots of friends, but none of them nice: she kept picking up impossible people. The Floyd-Taylors, with whom she had been at Boulogne, were simply horrid. The Hammond Synges were perhaps not so vulgar, but they had no conscience in their dealings with her.

"She knows what I think of them," said Mrs. Meldrum, "and indeed she knows what I think of most things."

"She shares that privilege with most of your friends!" I replied laughing.

"No doubt; but possibly to some of my friends it makes a little difference. That girl doesn't care a button. She knows best of all what I think of Flora Saunt."

"And what may your opinion be?"

"Why, that she's not worth troubling about—an idiot too abysmal."

"Doesn't she care for that?"

"Just enough, as you saw, to hug me till I cry out. She's too pleased with herself for anything else to matter."

"Surely, my dear friend," I rejoined, "she has a good deal to be pleased with!"

"So every one tells her, and so you would have told her if I had given you the chance. However, that doesn't signify either, for her vanity is beyond all making or mending. She believes in herself, and she's welcome, after all, poor dear, having only herself to look to. I've seldom met a young woman more completely free to be silly. She has a clear course—she'll make a showy finish."

"Well," I replied, "as she probably will reduce many persons to the same degraded state, her partaking of it won't stand out so much."

"If you mean that the world's full of twaddlers I quite agree with you!" cried Mrs. Meldrum, trumpeting her laugh half across the Channel.

I had after this to consider a little what she would call my mother's son, but I didn't let it prevent me from insisting on her making me acquainted with Flora Saunt; indeed I took the bull by the horns, urging that she had drawn the portrait of a nature which common charity now demanded of her to put into relation with a character really fine. Such a frail creature was just an object of pity. This contention on my part had at first of course been jocular; but strange to say it was quite the ground I found myself taking with regard to our young lady after I had begun to know her. I couldn't have said what I felt about her except that she was undefended; from the first of my sitting with her there after dinner, under the stars—that was a week at Folkestone of balmy nights and muffled tides and crowded chairs—I became aware both that protection was wholly absent from her life and that she was wholly indifferent to its absence. The odd thing was that she was not appealing: she was abjectly, divinely conceited, absurdly fantastically pleased. Her beauty was as yet all the world to her, a world she had plenty to do to live in. Mrs. Meldrum told me more about her, and there was nothing that, as the centre of a group of giggling, nudging spectators, Flora wasn't ready to tell about herself. She held her little court in the crowd, upon the grass, playing her light over Jews and Gentiles, completely at ease in all promiscuities. It was an effect of these things that from the very first, with every one listening, I could mention that my main business with her would be just to have a go at her head and to arrange in that view for an early sitting. It would have been as impossible, I think, to be impertinent to her as it would have been to throw a stone at a plate-glass window; so any talk that went forward on the basis of her loveliness was the most natural thing in the world and immediately became the most general and sociable. It was when I saw all this that I judged how, though it was the last thing she asked for, what one would ever most have at her service was a curious compassion. That sentiment was coloured by the vision of the dire exposure of a being whom vanity had put so off her guard. Hers was the only vanity I have ever known that made its possessor superlatively soft. Mrs. Meldrum's further information contributed moreover to these indulgences—her account of the girl's neglected childhood and queer continental relegations, with straying squabbling Monte-Carlo-haunting parents; the more invidious picture, above all, of her pecuniary arrangement, still in force, with the Hammond Synges, who really, though they never took her out—practically she went out alone—had their hands half the time in her pocket. She had to pay for everything, down to her share of the wine-bills and the horses' fodder, down to Bertie Hammond Synge's fare in the "underground" when he went to the City for her. She had been left with just money enough to turn her head; and it hadn't even been put in trust, nothing prudent or proper had been done with it. She could spend her capital, and at the rate she was going, expensive, extravagant and with a swarm of parasites to help, it certainly wouldn't last very long.

"Couldn't *you* perhaps take her, independent, unencumbered as you are?" I asked of Mrs. Meldrum. "You're probably, with one exception, the sanest person she knows, and you at least wouldn't scandalously fleece her."

"How do you know what I wouldn't do?" my humorous friend demanded. "Of course I've thought how I can help her—it has kept me awake at night. But doing it's impossible; she'll take nothing from me. You know what she does—she hugs me and runs away. She has an instinct about me and feels that I've one about her. And then she dislikes me for another reason that I'm not quite clear about, but that I'm well aware of and that I shall find out some day. So far as her settling with me goes it would be impossible moreover here; she wants naturally enough a much wider field. She must live in London—her game is there. So she takes the line of adoring me, of saying she can never forget that I was devoted to her mother—which I wouldn't for the world have been—and of giving me a wide berth. I think she positively dislikes to look at me. It's all right; there's no obligation; though people in general can't take their eyes off me."

"I see that at this moment," I replied. "But what does it matter where or how, for the present, she lives? She'll marry infallibly, marry early, and everything then will change."

"Whom will she marry?" my companion gloomily asked.

"Any one she likes. She's so abnormally pretty that she can do anything. She'll fascinate some nabob or some prince."

"She'll fascinate him first and bore him afterwards. Moreover she's not so pretty as you make her out; she hasn't a scrap of a figure."

"No doubt, but one doesn't in the least miss it."

"Not now," said Mrs. Meldrum, "but one will when she's older and when everything will have to count."

"When she's older she'll count as a princess, so it won't matter."

"She has other drawbacks," my companion went on. "Those wonderful eyes are good for nothing but to roll about like sugar-balls—which they greatly resemble—in a child's mouth. She can't use them."

"Use them? Why, she does nothing else."

"To make fools of young men, but not to read or write, not to do any sort of work. She never opens a book, and her maid writes her notes. You'll say that those who live in glass houses shouldn't throw stones. Of course I know that if I didn't wear my goggles I shouldn't be good for much."

"Do you mean that Miss Saunt ought to sport such things?" I exclaimed with more horror than I meant to show.

"I don't prescribe for her; I don't know that they're what she requires."

"What's the matter with her eyes?" I asked after a moment.

"I don't exactly know; but I heard from her mother years ago that even as a child they had had for a while to put her into spectacles and that though she hated them and had been in a fury of disgust, she would always have to be extremely careful. I'm sure I hope she is!"

I echoed the hope, but I remember well the impression this made upon me—my immediate pang of resentment, a disgust almost equal to Flora's own. I felt as if a great rare sapphire had split in my hand.

CHAPTER III

This conversation occurred the night before I went back to town. I settled on the morrow to take a late train, so that I had still my morning to spend at Folkestone, where during the greater part of it I was out with my mother. Every one in the place was as usual out with some one else, and even had I been free to go and take leave of her I should have been sure that Flora Saunt would not be at home. Just where she was I presently discovered: she was at the far end of the cliff, the point at which it overhangs the pretty view of Sandgate and Hythe. Her back, however, was turned to this attraction; it rested with the aid of her elbows, thrust slightly behind her so that her scanty little shoulders were raised toward her ears, on the high rail that inclosed the down. Two gentlemen stood before her whose faces we couldn't see but who even as observed from the rear were visibly absorbed in the charming figure-piece submitted to them. I was freshly struck with the fact that this meagre and defective little person, with the cock of her hat and the flutter of her crape, with her eternal idleness, her eternal happiness, her absence of moods and mysteries and the pretty presentation of her feet, which especially now in the supported slope of her posture occupied with their imperceptibility so much of the foreground—I was reminded anew, I say, how our young lady dazzled by some art that the enumeration of her merits didn't explain and that the mention of her lapses didn't affect. Where she was amiss nothing counted, and where she was right everything did. I say she was wanting in mystery, but that after all was her secret. This happened to be my first chance of introducing her to my mother, who had not much left in life but the quiet look from under the hood of her chair at the things which, when she should have quitted those she loved, she could still trust to make the world good for them. I wondered an instant how much she might be moved to trust Flora Saunt, and then while the chair stood still and she waited I went over and asked the girl to come and speak to her. In this way I saw that if one of Flora's attendants was the inevitable young Hammond Synge, master of ceremonies of her regular court, always offering the use of a telescope and accepting that of a cigar, the other was a personage I had not yet encountered, a small pale youth in showy knickerbockers, whose eyebrows and nose and the glued points of whose little moustache were extraordinarily uplifted and sustained. I remember taking him at first for a foreigner and for something of a pretender: I scarce know why unless because of the motive I felt in the stare he fixed on me when I asked Miss Saunt to come away. He struck me a little as a young man practising the social art of impertinence; but it didn't matter, for Flora came away with alacrity, bringing all her prettiness and pleasure and gliding over the grass in that rustle of delicate mourning which made the endless variety of her garments, as a painter could take heed, strike one always as the same obscure elegance. She seated herself on the floor of my mother's chair, a little too much on her right instep as I afterwards gathered, caressing her still hand, smiling up into her cold face, commending and approving her without a reserve and without a doubt. She told her immediately, as if it were something for her to hold on by, that she was soon to sit to me for a "likeness," and these words gave me a chance to enquire if it would be the fate of the picture, should I finish it, to be presented to the young man in the knickerbockers. Her lips, at this, parted in a stare; her eyes darkened to the purple of one of the shadow-patches on the sea. She showed for the passing instant the face of some splendid tragic mask, and I remembered for the inconsequence of it what Mrs. Meldrum had said about her sight. I had derived from this lady a worrying impulse to catechise her, but that didn't seem exactly kind; so I substituted another question, inquiring who the pretty young man in knickerbockers might happen to be.

"Oh a gentleman I met at Boulogne. He has come over to see me." After a moment she added: "Lord Iffield."

I had never heard of Lord Iffield, but her mention of his having been at Boulogne helped me to give him a niche. Mrs. Meldrum had incidentally thrown a certain light on the manners of Mrs. Floyd-Taylor, Flora's recent hostess in that charming town, a lady who, it appeared, had a special vocation for helping rich young men to find a use for their leisure. She had always one or other in hand and had apparently on this occasion pointed her lesson at the rare creature on the opposite coast. I had a vague idea that Boulogne was not a resort of the world's envied; at the same time there might very well have been a strong attraction there even for one of the darlings of fortune. I could perfectly understand in any case that such a darling should be drawn to Folkestone by Flora Saunt. But it was not in truth of these things I was thinking; what was uppermost in my mind was a matter which, though it had no sort of keeping, insisted just then on coming out.

"Is it true, Miss Saunt," I suddenly demanded, "that you're so unfortunate as to have had some warning about your beautiful eyes?"

I was startled by the effect of my words; the girl threw back her head, changing colour from brow to chin. "True? Who in the world says so?" I repented of my question in a flash; the way she met it made it seem cruel, and I felt my mother look at me in some surprise. I took care, in answer to Flora's challenge, not to incriminate Mrs. Meldrum. I answered that the rumour had reached me only in the vaguest form and that if I had been moved to put it to the test my very real interest in her must be held responsible. Her blush died away, but a pair of still prettier tears glistened in its track. "If you ever hear such a thing said again you can say it's a horrid lie!" I had brought on a commotion deeper than any I was prepared for; but it was explained in some degree by the next words she uttered: "I'm happy to say there's nothing the matter with any part of me whatever, not the least little thing!" She spoke with her habitual complacency, with triumphant assurance; she smiled again, and I could see how she wished that she hadn't so taken me up. She turned it off with a laugh. "I've good eyes, good teeth, a good digestion and a good temper. I'm sound of wind and limb!" Nothing could have been more characteristic than her blush and her tears, nothing less acceptable to her than to be thought not perfect in every particular. She couldn't submit to the imputation of a flaw. I expressed my delight in what she told me, assuring her I should always do battle for her; and as if to rejoin her companions she got up from her place on my mother's toes. The young men presented their backs to us; they were leaning on the rail of the cliff. Our incident had produced a certain awkwardness, and while I was thinking of what next to say she exclaimed irrelevantly: "Don't you know? He'll be Lord Considine." At that moment the youth marked for this high destiny turned round, and she spoke to my mother. "I'll introduce him to you—he's awfully nice." She beckoned and invited him with her parasol; the movement struck me as taking everything for granted. I had heard of Lord Considine and if I had not been able to place Lord Iffield it was because I didn't know the name of his eldest son. The young man took no notice of Miss Saunt's appeal; he only stared a moment and then on her repeating it quietly turned his back. She was an odd creature: she didn't blush at this; she only said to my mother apologetically, but with the frankest sweetest amusement, "You don't mind, do you? He's a monster of shyness!" It was as if she were sorry for every one—for Lord Iffield, the victim of a complaint so painful, and for my mother, the subject of a certain slight. "I'm sure I don't want him!" said my mother, but Flora added some promise of how she would handle him for his rudeness. She would clearly never explain anything by any failure of her own appeal. There rolled over me while she took leave of us and floated back to her friends a wave of superstitious dread. I seemed somehow to see her go forth to her fate, and yet what should fill out this orb of a high destiny if not such beauty and such joy? I had a dim idea that Lord Considine was a great proprietor, and though there mingled with it a faint impression that I shouldn't like his son the result of the two images was a whimsical prayer that the girl mightn't miss her possible fortune.

CHAPTER IV

One day in the course of the following June there was ushered into my studio a gentleman whom I had not yet seen but with whom I had been very briefly in correspondence. A letter from him had expressed to me some days before his regret on learning that my "splendid portrait" of Miss Flora Louisa Saunt, whose full name figured by her own wish in the catalogue of the exhibition of the Academy, had found a purchaser before the close of the private view. He took the liberty of inquiring whether I might have at his service some other memorial of the same lovely head, some preliminary sketch, some study for the picture. I had replied that I had indeed painted Miss Saunt more than once and that if he were interested in my work I should be happy to show him what I had done. Mr. Geoffrey Dawling, the person thus introduced to me, stumbled into my room with awkward movements and equivocal sounds—a long, lean, confused, confusing young man, with a bad complexion and large protrusive teeth. He bore in its most indelible pressure the postmark, as it were, of Oxford, and as soon as he opened his mouth I perceived, in addition to a remarkable revelation of gums, that the text of the queer communication matched the registered envelope. He was full of refinements and angles, of dreary and distinguished knowledge. Of his unconscious drollery his dress freely partook; it seemed, from the gold ring into which his red necktie was passed to the square toe-caps of his boots, to conform with a high sense of modernness to the fashion before the last. There were moments when his overdone urbanity, all suggestive stammers and interrogative quavers, made him scarcely intelligible; but I felt him to be a gentleman and I liked the honesty of his errand and the expression of his good green eyes.

As a worshipper at the shrine of beauty, however, he needed explaining, especially when I found he had no acquaintance with my brilliant model; had on the mere evidence of my picture taken, as he said, a tremendous fancy to her looks. I ought doubtless to have been humiliated by the simplicity of his judgment of them, a judgment for which the rendering was lost in the subject, quite leaving out the element of art. He was like the innocent reader for whom the story is "really true" and the author a negligible quantity. He had come to me only because he wanted to purchase, and I remember being so amused at his attitude, which I had never seen equally marked in a person of education, that I asked him why, for the sort of enjoyment he desired, it wouldn't be more to the point to deal directly with the lady. He stared and blushed at this; the idea clearly alarmed him. He was an extraordinary case—personally so modest that I could see it had never occurred to him. He had fallen in love with a painted sign and seemed content just to dream of what it stood for. He was the young prince in the legend or the comedy who loses his heart to the miniature of the princess beyond seas. Until I knew him better this puzzled me much—the link was so missing between his sensibility and his type. He was of course bewildered by my sketches, which implied in the beholder some sense of intention and quality; but for one of them, a comparative failure, he ended by conceiving a preference so arbitrary and so lively that, taking no second look at the others, he expressed his wish to possess it and fell into the extremity of confusion over the question of price. I helped him over that stile, and he went off without having asked me a direct question about Miss Saunt, yet with his acquisition under his arm. His delicacy was such that he evidently considered his rights to be limited; he had acquired none at all in regard to the original of the picture. There were others—for I was curious about him—that I wanted him to feel I conceded: I should have been glad of his carrying away a sense of ground acquired for coming back. To ensure this I had probably only to invite him, and I perfectly recall the impulse that made me forbear. It operated suddenly from within while he hung about the door and in spite of the diffident appeal that blinked in his gentle grin. If he was smitten with Flora's ghost what mightn't be the direct force of the luminary that could cast such a shadow? This source of radiance, flooding my poor place, might very well happen to be present the next time he should turn up. The idea was sharp within me that there were relations and complications it was no mission of mine to bring about. If they were to develop they should develop in their very own sense.

Let me say at once that they did develop and that I perhaps after all had something to do with it. If Mr. Dawling had departed without a fresh appointment he was to reappear six months later under protection no less powerful than that of our young lady herself. I had seen her repeatedly for months: she had grown to regard my studio as the temple of her beauty. This miracle was recorded and celebrated there as nowhere else; in other places there was occasional reference to other subjects of remark. The degree of her presumption continued to be stupefying; there was nothing so extraordinary save the degree in which she never paid for it. She was kept innocent, that is she was kept safe, by her egotism, but she was helped also, though she had now put off her mourning, by the attitude of the lone orphan who had to be a law unto herself. It was as a lone orphan that she came and went, as a lone orphan that she was the centre of a crush. The neglect of the Hammond Synges gave relief to this character, and she made it worth their while to be, as every one said, too shocking. Lord Iffield had gone to India to shoot tigers, but he returned in time for the punctual private view: it was he who had snapped up, as Flora called it, the gem of the exhibition. My hope for the girl's future had slipped ignominiously off his back, but after his purchase of the portrait I tried to cultivate a new faith. The girl's own faith was wonderful. It couldn't however be contagious: too great was the limit of her sense of what painters call values. Her colours were laid on like blankets on a cold night. How indeed could a person speak the truth who was always posturing and bragging? She was after all vulgar enough, and by the time I had mastered her profile and could almost with my eyes shut do it in a single line I was decidedly tired of its "purity," which affected me at last as inane. One moved with her, moreover, among phenomena mismated and unrelated; nothing in her talk ever matched anything out of it. Lord Iffield was dying of love for her, but his family was leading him a life. His mother, horrid woman, had told some one that she would rather he should be swallowed by a tiger than marry a girl not absolutely one of themselves. He had given his young friend unmistakable signs, but was lying low, gaining time: it was in his father's power to be, both in personal and in pecuniary ways, excessively nasty to him. His father wouldn't last for ever—quite the contrary; and he knew how thoroughly, in spite of her youth, her beauty and the swarm of her admirers, some of them positively threatening in their passion, he could trust her to hold out. There were richer, cleverer men, there were greater personages too, but she liked her "little viscount" just as he was, and liked to think that, bullied and persecuted, he had her there so gratefully to rest upon. She came back to me with tale upon tale, and it all might be or mightn't. I never met my pretty model in the world—she moved, it appeared, in exalted circles—and could only admire, in her wealth of illustration, the grandeur of her life and the freedom of her hand.

I had on the first opportunity spoken to her of Geoffrey Dawling, and she had listened to my story so far as she had the art of such patience, asking me indeed more questions about him than I could answer; then she had capped my anecdote with others much more striking, the disclosure of effects produced in the most extraordinary quarters: on people who had followed her into railway carriages; guards and porters even who had literally stuck there; others who had spoken to her in shops and hung about her house door; cabmen, upon her honour, in London, who, to gaze their fill at her, had found excuses to thrust their petrifaction through the very glasses of four-wheelers. She lost herself in these reminiscences, the moral of which was that poor Mr. Dawling was only one of a million. When therefore the next autumn she flourished into my studio with her odd companion at her heels her first care was to make clear to me that if he was now in servitude it wasn't because she had run after him. Dawling explained with a hundred grins that when one wished very much to get anything one usually ended by doing so—a proposition which led me wholly to dissent and our young lady to asseverate that she hadn't in the least wished to get Mr. Dawling. She mightn't have wished to get him, but she wished to show him, and I seemed to read that if she could treat him as a trophy her affairs were rather at the ebb. True there always hung from her belt a promiscuous fringe of scalps. Much at any rate would have come and gone since our separation in July. She had spent four months abroad, where, on Swiss and Italian lakes, in German cities, in the French capital, many accidents might have happened.

CHAPTER V

I had been again with my mother, but except Mrs. Meldrum and the gleam of France had not found at Folkestone my old resources and pastimes. Mrs. Meldrum, much edified by my report of the performances, as she called them, in my studio, had told me that to her knowledge Flora would soon be on the straw: she had cut from her capital such fine fat slices that there was almost nothing more left to swallow. Perched on her breezy cliff the good lady dazzled me as usual by her universal light: she knew so much more about everything and everybody than I could ever squeeze out of my colour-tubes. She knew that Flora was acting on system and absolutely declined to be interfered with: her precious reasoning was that her money would last as long as she should need it, that a magnificent marriage would crown her charms before she should be really pinched. She had a sum put by for a liberal outfit; meanwhile the proper use of the rest was to decorate her for the approaches to the altar, keep her afloat in the society in which she would most naturally meet her match. Lord Iffield had been seen with her at Lucerne, at Cadenabbia; but it was Mrs. Meldrum's conviction that nothing was to be expected of him but the most futile flirtation. The girl had a certain hold of him, but with a great deal of swagger he hadn't the spirit of a sheep: he was in fear of his father and would never commit himself in Lord Considine's lifetime. The most Flora might achieve was that he wouldn't marry some one else. Geoffrey Dawling, to Mrs. Meldrum's knowledge (I had told her of the young man's visit) had attached himself on the way back from Italy to the Hammond Synge group. My informant was in a position to be definite about this dangler; she knew about his people; she had heard of him before. Hadn't he been a friend of one of her nephews at Oxford? Hadn't he spent the Christmas holidays precisely three years before at her brother-in-law's in Yorkshire, taking that occasion to get himself refused with derision by wilful Betty, the second daughter of the house? Her sister, who liked the floundering youth, had written to her to complain of Betty, and that the young man should now turn up as an appendage of Flora's was one of those oft-cited proofs that the world is small and that there are not enough people to go round. His father had been something or other in the Treasury; his grandfather on the mother's side had been something or other in the Church. He had come into the paternal estate, two or three thousand a year in Hampshire; but he had let the place advantageously and was generous to four plain sisters who lived at Bournemouth and adored him. The family was hideous all round, but the very salt of the earth. He was supposed to be unspeakably clever; he was fond of London, fond of books, of intellectual society and of the idea of a political career. That such a man should be at the same time fond of Flora Saunt attested, as the phrase in the first volume of Gibbon has it, the variety of his inclinations. I was soon to learn that he was fonder of her than of all the other things together. Betty, one of five and with views above her station, was at any rate felt at home to have dished herself by her perversity. Of course no one had looked at her since and no one would ever look at her again. It would be eminently desirable that Flora should learn the lesson of Betty's fate.

I was not struck, I confess, with all this in my mind, by any symptom on our young lady's part of that sort of meditation. The one moral she saw in anything was that of her incomparable aspect, which Mr. Dawling, smitten even like the railway porters and the cabmen by the doom-dealing gods, had followed from London to Venice and from Venice back to London again. I afterwards learned that her version of this episode was profusely inexact: his personal acquaintance with her had been determined by an accident remarkable enough, I admit, in connexion with what had gone before—a coincidence at all events superficially striking. At Munich, returning from a tour in the Tyrol with two of his sisters, he had found himself at the table d'hôte of his inn opposite to the full presentment of that face of which the mere clumsy copy had made him dream and desire. He had been tossed by it to a height so vertiginous as to involve a retreat from the board; but the next day he had dropped with a resounding thud at the very feet of his apparition. On the following, with an equal incoherence, a sacrifice even of his bewildered sisters, whom he left behind, he made an heroic effort to escape by flight from a fate of which he had already felt the cold breath. That fate, in London, very little later, drove him straight before it—drove him one Sunday afternoon, in the rain, to the door of the Hammond Synges. He marched in other words close up to the cannon that was to blow him to pieces. But three weeks, when he reappeared to me, had elapsed since then, yet (to vary my metaphor) the burden he was to carry for the rest of his days was firmly lashed to his back. I don't mean by this that Flora had been persuaded to contract her scope; I mean that he had been treated to the unconditional snub which, as the event was to show, couldn't have been bettered as a means of securing him. She hadn't calculated, but she had said "Never!" and that word had made a bed big enough for his long-legged patience. He became from this moment to my mind the interesting figure in the piece.

Now that he had acted without my aid I was free to show him this, and having on his own side something to show me he repeatedly knocked at my door. What he brought with him on these occasions was a simplicity so huge that, as I turn my ear to the past, I seem even now to hear it bumping up and down my stairs. That was really what I saw of him in the light of his behaviour. He had fallen in love as he might have broken his leg, and the fracture was of a sort that would make him permanently lame. It was the whole man who limped and lurched, with nothing of him left in the same position as before. The tremendous cleverness, the literary society, the political ambition, the Bournemouth sisters all seemed to flop with his every movement a little nearer to the floor. I hadn't had an Oxford training and I had never encountered the great man at whose feet poor Dawling had most submissively sat and who had addressed him his most destructive sniffs; but I remember asking myself how effectively this privilege had supposed itself to prepare him for the career on which my friend appeared now to have embarked. I remember too making up my mind about the cleverness, which had its uses and I suppose in impenetrable shades even its critics, but from which the friction of mere personal intercourse was not the sort of process to extract a revealing spark. He accepted without a question both his fever and his chill, and the only thing he touched with judgment was this convenience of my friendship. He doubtless told me his simple story, but the matter comes back in a kind of sense of my being rather the mouthpiece, of my having had to put it together for him. He took it from me in this form without a groan, and I gave it him quite as it came; he took it again and again, spending his odd half-hours with me as if for the very purpose of learning how idiotically he was in love. He told me I made him see things: to begin with, hadn't I first made him see Flora Saunt? I wanted him to give her up and lucidly informed him why; on which he never protested nor contradicted, never was even so alembicated as to declare just for the sake of the point that he wouldn't. He simply and pointlessly didn't, and when at the end of three months I asked him what was the use of talking with such a fellow his nearest approach to a justification was to say that what made him want to help her was just the deficiencies I dwelt on. I could only reply without gross developments: "Oh if you're as sorry for her as that!" I too was nearly as sorry for her as that, but it only led me to be sorrier still for other victims of this compassion. With Dawling as with me the compassion was at first in excess of any visible motive; so that when eventually the motive was supplied each could to a certain extent compliment the other on the fineness of his foresight.

After he had begun to haunt my studio Miss Saunt quite gave it up, and I finally learned that she accused me of conspiring with him to put pressure on her to marry him. She didn't know I would take it that way, else she would never have brought him to see me. It was in her view a part of the conspiracy that to show him a kindness I asked him at last to sit to me. I dare say moreover she was disgusted to hear that I had ended by attempting almost as many sketches of his beauty as I had attempted of hers. What was the value of tributes to beauty by a hand that could so abase itself? My relation to poor Dawling's want of modelling was simple enough. I was really digging in that sandy desert for the buried treasure of his soul.

CHAPTER VI

It befell at this period, just before Christmas, that on my having gone under pressure of the season into a great shop to buy a toy or two, my eyes fleeing from superfluity, lighted at a distance on the bright concretion of Flora Saunt, an exhibitability that held its own even against the most plausible pinkness of the most developed dolls. A huge quarter of the place, the biggest bazaar "on earth," was peopled with these and other effigies and fantasies, as well as with purchasers and vendors haggard alike, in the blaze of the gas, with hesitations. I was just about to appeal to Flora to avert that stage of my errand when I saw that she was accompanied by a gentleman whose identity, though more than a year had elapsed, came back to me from the Folkestone cliff. It had been associated on that scene with showy knickerbockers; at present it overflowed more splendidly into a fur-trimmed overcoat. Lord Iffield's presence made me waver an instant before crossing over, and during that instant Flora, blank and undistinguishing, as if she too were after all weary of alternatives, looked straight across at me. I was on the point of raising my hat to her when I observed that her face gave no sign. I was exactly in the line of her vision, but she either didn't see me or didn't recognise me, or else had a reason to pretend she didn't. Was her reason that I had displeased her and that she wished to punish me? I had always thought it one of her merits that she wasn't vindictive. She at any rate simply looked away; and at this moment one of the shop-girls, who had apparently gone off in search of it, bustled up to her with a small mechanical toy. It so happened that I followed closely what then took place, afterwards recognising that I had been led to do so, led even through the crowd to press nearer for the purpose, by an impression of which in the act I was not fully conscious.

Flora with the toy in her hand looked round at her companion; then seeing his attention had been solicited in another quarter she moved away with the shop-girl, who had evidently offered to conduct her into the presence of more objects of the same sort. When she reached the indicated spot I was in a position still to observe her. She had asked some question about the working of the toy, and the girl, taking it herself, began to explain the little secret. Flora bent her head over it, but she clearly didn't understand. I saw her, in a manner that quickened my curiosity, give a glance back at the place from which she had come. Lord Iffield was talking with another young person; she satisfied herself of this by the aid of a question addressed to her own attendant. She then drew closer to the table near which she stood and, turning her back to me, bent her head lower over the collection of toys and more particularly over the small object the girl had attempted to explain. She took it again and, after a moment, with her face well averted, made an odd motion of her arms and a significant little duck of her head. These slight signs, singular as it may appear, produced in my bosom an agitation so great that I failed to notice Lord Iffield's whereabouts. He had rejoined her; he was close upon her before I knew it or before she knew it herself. I felt at that instant the strangest of all promptings: if it could have operated more rapidly it would have caused me to dash between them in some such manner as to give Flora a caution. In fact as it was I think I could have done this in time had I not been checked by a curiosity stronger still than my impulse. There were three seconds during which I saw the young man and yet let him come on. Didn't I make the quick calculation that if he didn't catch what Flora was doing I too might perhaps not catch it? She at any rate herself took the alarm. On perceiving her companion's nearness she made, still averted, another duck of her head and a shuffle of her hands so precipitate that a little tin steamboat she had been holding escaped from them and rattled down to the floor with a sharpness that I hear at this hour. Lord Iffield had already seized her arm; with a violent jerk he brought her round toward him. Then it was that there met my eyes a quite distressing sight: this exquisite creature, blushing, glaring, exposed, with a pair of big black-rimmed eye-glasses, defacing her by their position, crookedly astride of her beautiful nose. She made a grab at them with her free hand while I turned confusedly away.

CHAPTER VII

I don't remember how soon it was I spoke to Geoffrey Dawling; his sittings were irregular, but it was certainly the very next time he gave me one.

"Has any rumour ever reached you of Miss Saunt's having anything the matter with her eyes?" He stared with a candour that was a sufficient answer to my question, backing it up with a shocked and mystified "Never!" Then I asked him if he had observed in her any symptom, however disguised, of embarrassed sight; on which, after a moment's thought, he exclaimed "Disguised?" as if my use of that word had vaguely awakened a train. "She's not a bit myopic," he said; "she doesn't blink or contract her lids." I fully recognised this and I mentioned that she altogether denied the impeachment; owing it to him moreover to explain the ground of my inquiry, I gave him a sketch of the incident that had taken place before me at the shop. He knew all about Lord Iffield; that nobleman had figured freely in our conversation as his preferred, his injurious rival. Poor Dawling's contention was that if there had been a definite engagement between his lordship and the young lady, the sort of thing that was announced in the Morning Post, renunciation and retirement would be comparatively easy to him; but that having waited in vain for any such assurance he was entitled to act as if the door were not really closed or were at any rate not cruelly locked. He was naturally much struck with my anecdote and still more with my interpretation of it.

"There *is* something, there *is* something—possibly something very grave, certainly something that requires she should make use of artificial aids. She won't admit it publicly, because with her idolatry of her beauty, the feeling she is all made up of, she sees in such aids nothing but the humiliation and the disfigurement. She has used them in secret, but that is evidently not enough, for the affection she suffers from, apparently some definite menace, has lately grown much worse. She looked straight at me in the shop, which was violently lighted, without seeing it was I. At the same distance, at Folkestone, where as you know I first met her, where I heard this mystery hinted at and where she indignantly denied the thing, she appeared easily enough to recognise people At present she couldn't really make out anything the shop-girl showed her She has successfully concealed from the man I saw her with that she resorts in private to a pince-nez and that she does so not only under the strictest orders from her oculist, but because literally the poor thing can't accomplish without such help half the business of life. Iffield however has suspected something and his suspicions, whether expressed or kept to himself, have put him on the watch. I happened to have a glimpse of the movement at which he pounced on her and caught her in the act."

I had thought it all out; my idea explained many things, and Dawling turned pale as he listened to me.

"Was he rough with her?" he anxiously asked.

"How can I tell what passed between them? I fled from the place."

My companion stared. "Do you mean to say her eyesight's going?"

"Heaven forbid! In that case how could she take life as she does?"

"How *does* she take life? That's the question!" He sat there bewilderedly brooding; the tears rose to his lids; they reminded me of those I had seen in Flora's the day I risked my enquiry. The question he had asked was one that to my own satisfaction I was ready to answer, but I hesitated to let him hear as yet all that my reflections had suggested. I was indeed privately astonished at their ingenuity. For the present I only rejoined that it struck me she was playing a particular game; at which he went on as if he hadn't heard me, suddenly haunted with a fear, lost in the dark possibility. "Do you mean there's a danger of anything very bad?"

"My dear fellow, you must ask her special adviser."

"Who in the world is her special adviser?"

"I haven't a conception. But we mustn't get too excited. My impression would be that she has only to observe a few ordinary rules, to exercise a little common sense."

Dawling jumped at this. "I see—to stick to the pince-nez."

"To follow to the letter her oculist's prescription, whatever it is and at whatever cost to her prettiness. It's not a thing to be trifled with."

"Upon my honour it *shan't* be!" he roundly declared; and he adjusted himself to his position again as if we had quite settled the business. After a considerable interval, while I botched away, he suddenly said: "Did they make a great difference?"

"A great difference?"

"Those things she had put on."

"Oh the glasses—in her beauty? She looked queer of course, but it was partly because one was unaccustomed. There are women who look charming in nippers. What, at any rate, if she does look queer? She must be mad not to accept that alternative."

"She *is* mad," said Geoffrey Dawling.

"Mad to refuse you, I grant. Besides," I went on, "the pince-nez, which was a large and peculiar one, was all awry: she had half pulled it off, but it continued to stick, and she was crimson, she was angry."

"It must have been horrible!" my companion groaned.

"It *was* horrible. But it's still more horrible to defy all warnings; it's still more horrible to be landed in—" Without saying in what I disgustedly shrugged my shoulders.

After a glance at me Dawling jerked round. "Then you do believe that she may be?"

I hesitated. "The thing would be to make *her* believe it. She only needs a good scare."

"But if that fellow is shocked at the precautions she does take?"

"Oh who knows?" I rejoined with small sincerity. "I don't suppose Iffield is absolutely a brute."

"I would take her with leather blinders, like a shying mare!" cried Geoffrey Dawling.

I had an impression that Iffield wouldn't, but I didn't communicate it, for I wanted to pacify my friend, whom I had discomposed too much for the purposes of my sitting. I recollect that I did some good work that morning, but it also comes back to me that before we separated he had practically revealed to me that my anecdote, connecting itself in his mind with a series of observations at the time unconscious and unregistered, had covered with light the subject of our colloquy. He had had a formless perception of some secret that drove Miss Saunt to subterfuges, and the more he thought of it the more he guessed this secret to be the practice of making believe she saw when she didn't and of cleverly keeping people from finding out how little she saw. When one pieced things together it was astonishing what ground they covered. Just as he was going away he asked me from what source at Folkestone the horrid tale had proceeded. When I had given him, as I saw no reason not to do, the name of Mrs. Meldrum he exclaimed: "Oh I know all about her; she's a friend of some friends of mine!" At this I remembered wilful Betty and said to myself that I knew some one who would probably prove more wilful still.

CHAPTER VIII

A few days later I again heard Dawling on my stairs, and even before he passed my threshold I knew he had something to tell.

"I've been down to Folkestone—it was necessary I should see her!" I forget whether he had come straight from the station; he was at any rate out of breath with his news, which it took me however a minute to apply.

"You mean that you've been with Mrs. Meldrum?"

"Yes, to ask her what she knows and how she comes to know it. It worked upon me awfully—I mean what you told me." He made a visible effort to seem quieter than he was, and it showed me sufficiently that he had not been reassured. I laid, to comfort him and smiling at a venture, a friendly hand on his arm, and he dropped into my eyes, fixing them an instant, a strange distended look which might have expressed the cold clearness of all that was to come. "I *know*—now!" he said with an emphasis he rarely used.

"What then did Mrs. Meldrum tell you?"

"Only one thing that signified, for she has no real knowledge. But that one thing was everything."

"What is it then?"

"Why, that she can't bear the sight of her." His pronouns required some arranging, but after I had successfully dealt with them I replied that I was quite aware of Miss Saunt's trick of turning her back on the good lady of Folkestone. Only what did that prove? "Have you never guessed? I guessed as soon as she spoke!" Dawling towered over me in dismal triumph. It was the first time in our acquaintance that, on any ground of understanding this had occurred; but even so remarkable an incident still left me sufficiently at sea to cause him to continue: "Why, the effect of those spectacles!"

I seemed to catch the tail of his idea. "Mrs. Meldrum's?"

"They're so awfully ugly and they add so to the dear woman's ugliness." This remark began to flash a light, and when he quickly added "She sees herself, she sees her own fate!" my response was so immediate that I had almost taken the words out of his mouth. While I tried to fix this sudden image of Flora's face glazed in and cross-barred even as Mrs. Meldrum's was glazed and barred, he went on to assert that only the horror of that image, looming out at herself, could be the reason of her avoiding the person who so forced it home. The fact he had encountered made everything hideously vivid, and more vivid than anything else that just such another pair of goggles was what would have been prescribed to Flora.

"I see—I see," I presently returned. "What would become of Lord Iffield if she were suddenly to come out in them? What indeed would become of every one, what would become of everything?" This was an enquiry that Dawling was evidently unprepared to meet, and I completed it by saying at last: "My dear fellow, for that matter, what would become of *you*?"

Once more he turned on me his good green eyes. "Oh I shouldn't mind!"

The tone of his words somehow made his ugly face beautiful, and I discovered at this moment how much I really liked him. None the less, at the same time, perversely and rudely, I felt the droll side of our discussion of such alternatives. It made me laugh out and say to him while I laughed: "You'd take her even with those things of Mrs. Meldrum's?"

He remained mournfully grave; I could see that he was surprised at my rude mirth. But he summoned back a vision of the lady at Folkestone and conscientiously replied: "Even with those things of Mrs. Meldrum's." I begged him not to resent my laughter, which but exposed the fact that we had built a monstrous castle in the air. Didn't he see on what flimsy ground the structure rested? The evidence was preposterously small. He believed the worst, but we were really uninformed.

"I shall find out the truth," he promptly replied.

"How can you? If you question her you'll simply drive her to perjure herself. Wherein after all does it concern you to know the truth? It's the girl's own affair."

"Then why did you tell me your story?"

I was a trifle embarrassed. "To warn you off," I smiled. He took no more notice of these words than presently to remark that Lord Iffield had no serious intentions. "Very possibly," I said. "But you mustn't speak as if Lord Iffield and you were her only alternatives."

Dawling thought a moment. "Couldn't something be got out of the people she has consulted? She must have been to people. How else can she have been condemned?"

"Condemned to what? Condemned to perpetual nippers? Of course she has consulted some of the big specialists, but she has done it, you may be sure, in the most clandestine manner; and even if it were supposable that they would tell you anything—which I altogether doubt—you would have great difficulty in finding out which men they are. Therefore leave it alone; never show her what you suspect."

I even before he quitted me asked him to promise me this. "All right, I promise"—but he was gloomy enough. He was a lover facing the fact that there was no limit to the deceit his loved one was ready to practise: it made so remarkably little difference. I could see by what a stretch his passionate pity would from this moment overlook the girl's fatuity and folly. She was always accessible to him—that I knew; for if she had told him he was an idiot to dream she could dream of him, she would have rebuked the imputation of having failed to make it clear that she would always be glad to regard him as a friend. What were most of her friends—what were all of them—but repudiated idiots? I was perfectly aware that in her conversations and confidences I myself for instance had a niche in the gallery. As regards poor Dawling I knew how often he still called on the Hammond Synges. It was not there but under the wing of the Floyd-Taylors that her intimacy with Lord Iffield most flourished. At all events, when a week after the visit I have just summarised Flora's name was one morning brought up to me, I jumped at the conclusion that Dawling had been with her, and even I fear briefly entertained the thought that he had broken his word.

CHAPTER IX

She left me, after she had been introduced, in no suspense about her present motive; she was on the contrary in a visible fever to enlighten me, but I promptly learned that for the alarm with which she pitiably panted our young man was not accountable. She had but one thought in the world, and that thought was for Lord Iffield. I had the strangest saddest scene with her, and if it did me no other good it at least made me at last completely understand why insidiously, from the first, she had struck me as a creature of tragedy. In showing me the whole of her folly it lifted the curtain of her misery. I don't know how much she meant to tell me when she came—I think she had had plans of elaborate misrepresentation; at any rate she found it at the end of ten minutes the simplest way to break down and sob, to be wretched and true. When she had once begun to let herself go the movement took her off her feet; the relief of it was like the cessation of a cramp. She shared in a word her long secret, she shifted her sharp pain. She brought, I confess, tears to my own eyes, tears of helpless tenderness for her helpless poverty. Her visit however was not quite so memorable in itself as in some of its consequences, the most immediate of which was that I went that afternoon to see Geoffrey Dawling, who had in those days rooms in Welbeck Street, where I presented myself at an hour late enough to warrant the supposition that he might have come in. He had not come in, but he was expected, and I was invited to enter and wait for him: a lady, I was informed, was already in his sitting-room. I hesitated, a little at a loss: it had wildly coursed through my brain that the lady was perhaps Flora Saunt. But when I asked if she were young and remarkably pretty I received so significant a "No sir!" that I risked an advance and after a minute in this manner found myself, to my astonishment, face to face with Mrs. Meldrum.

"Oh you dear thing," she exclaimed, "I'm delighted to see you: you spare me another compromising démarche! But for this I should have called on you also. Know the worst at once: if you see me here it's at least deliberate—it's planned, plotted, shameless. I came up on purpose to see him, upon my word I'm in love with him. Why, if you valued my peace of mind, did you let him the other day at Folkestone dawn upon my delighted eyes? I found myself there in half an hour simply infatuated with him. With a perfect sense of everything that can be urged against him I hold him none the less the very pearl of men. However, I haven't come up to declare my passion—I've come to bring him news that will interest him much more. Above all I've come to urge upon him to be careful."

"About Flora Saunt?"

"About what he says and does: he must be as still as a mouse! She's at last really engaged."

"But it's a tremendous secret?" I was moved to mirth.

"Precisely: she wired me this noon, and spent another shilling to tell me that not a creature in the world is yet to know it."

"She had better have spent it to tell you that she had just passed an hour with the creature you see before you."

"She has just passed an hour with every one in the place!" Mrs. Meldrum cried. "They've vital reasons, she says, for it's not coming out for a month. Then it will be formally announced, but meanwhile her rejoicing is wild. I daresay Mr. Dawling already knows and, as it's nearly seven o'clock, may have jumped off London Bridge. But an effect of the talk I had with him the other day was to make me, on receipt of my telegram, feel it to be my duty to warn him in person against taking action, so to call it, on the horrid certitude which I could see he carried away with him. I had added somehow to that certitude. He told me what you had told him you had seen in your shop."

Mrs. Meldrum, I perceived, had come to Welbeck Street on an errand identical with my own—a circumstance indicating her rare sagacity, inasmuch as her ground for undertaking it was a very different thing from what Flora's wonderful visit had made of mine. I remarked to her that what I had seen in the shop was sufficiently striking, but that I had seen a great deal more that morning in my studio. "In short," I said, "I've seen everything."

She was mystified. "Everything?"

"The poor creature is under the darkest of clouds. Oh she came to triumph, but she remained to talk something in the nature of sense! She put herself completely in my hands—she does me the honour to intimate that of all her friends I'm the most disinterested. After she had announced to me that Lord Iffield was utterly committed to her and that for the present I was absolutely the only person in the secret, she arrived at her real business. She had had a suspicion of me ever since that day at Folkestone when I asked her for the truth about her eyes. The truth is what you and I both guessed. She's in very bad danger."

"But from what cause? I, who by God's mercy have kept mine, know everything that can be known about eyes," said Mrs. Meldrum.

"She might have kept hers if she had profited by God's mercy, if she had done in time, done years ago, what was imperatively ordered her; if she hadn't in fine been cursed with the loveliness that was to make her behaviour a thing of fable. She may still keep her sight, or what remains of it, if she'll sacrifice—and after all so little—that purely superficial charm. She must do as you've done; she must wear, dear lady, what you wear!"

What my companion wore glittered for the moment like a melon-frame in August. "Heaven forgive her—now I understand!" She flushed for dismay.

But I wasn't afraid of the effect on her good nature of her thus seeing, through her great goggles, why it had always been that Flora held her at such a distance. "I can't tell you," I said, "from what special affection, what state of the eye, her danger proceeds: that's the one thing she succeeded this morning in keeping from me. She knows it herself perfectly; she has had the best advice in Europe. 'It's a thing that's awful, simply awful'—that was the only account she would give me. Year before last, while she was at Boulogne, she went for three days with Mrs. Floyd-Taylor to Paris. She there surreptitiously consulted the greatest man—even Mrs. Floyd-Taylor doesn't know. Last autumn in Germany she did the same. 'First put on certain special spectacles with a straight bar in the middle: then we'll talk'—that's practically what they say. What *she* says is that she'll put on anything in nature when she's married, but that she must get married first. She has always meant to do everything as soon as she's married. Then and then only she'll be safe. How will any one ever look at her if she makes herself a fright? How could she ever have got engaged if she had made herself a fright from the first? It's no use to insist that with her beauty she can never *be* a fright. She said to me this morning, poor girl, the most characteristic, the most harrowing things. 'My face is all I have—and *such* a face! I knew from the first I could do anything with it. But I needed it all—I need it still, every exquisite inch of it. It isn't as if I had a figure or anything else. Oh if God had only given me a figure too, I don't say! Yes, with a figure, a really good one, like Fanny Floyd-Taylor's, who's hideous, I'd have risked plain glasses. Que voulez-vous? No one is perfect.' She says she still has money left, but I don't believe a word of it. She has been speculating on her impunity, on the idea that her danger would hold off: she has literally been running a race with it. Her theory has been, as you from the first so clearly saw, that she'd get in ahead. She swears to me that though the 'bar' is too cruel she wears when she's alone what she has been ordered to wear. But when the deuce is she alone? It's herself of course that she has swindled worst: she has put herself off, so insanely that even her conceit but half accounts for it, with little inadequate concessions, little false measures and preposterous evasions and childish hopes. Her great terror is now that Iffield, who already has suspicions, who has found out her pince-nez but whom she has beguiled with some unblushing hocus-pocus, may discover the dreadful facts; and the essence of what she wanted this morning was in that interest to square me, to get me to deny indignantly and authoritatively (for isn't she my 'favourite sitter?') that she has anything in life the matter with any part of her. She sobbed, she 'went on,' she entreated; after we got talking her extraordinary nerve left her and she showed me what she has been through—showed me also all her terror of the harm I could do her. 'Wait till I'm married! wait till I'm married!' She took hold of me, she almost sank on her knees. It seems to me highly immoral, one's participation in her fraud; but there's no doubt that she must be married: I don't know what I don't see behind it! Therefore," I wound up, "Dawling must keep his hands off."

Mrs. Meldrum had held her breath; she gave out a long moan. "Well, that's exactly what I came here to tell him."

"Then here he is." Our host, all unprepared, his latchkey still in his hand, had just pushed open the door and, startled at finding us, turned a frightened look from one to the other, wondering what disaster we were there to announce or avert.

Mrs. Meldrum was on the spot all gaiety. "I've come to return your sweet visit. Ah," she laughed, "I mean to keep up the acquaintance!"

"Do—do," he murmured mechanically and absently, continuing to look at us. Then he broke out: "He's going to marry her."

I was surprised. "You already know?"

He produced an evening paper, which he tossed down on the table. "It's in that."

"Published—already?" I was still more surprised.

"Oh Flora can't keep a secret!"—Mrs. Meldrum made it light. She went up to poor Dawling and laid a motherly hand upon him.

"It's all right—it's just as it ought to be: don't think about her ever any more." Then as he met this adjuration with a stare from which thought, and of the most defiant and dismal, fairly protruded, the excellent woman put up her funny face and tenderly kissed him on the cheek.

CHAPTER X

I have spoken of these reminiscences as of a row of coloured beads, and I confess that as I continue to straighten out my chaplet I am rather proud of the comparison. The beads are all there, as I said—they slip along the string in their small smooth roundness. Geoffrey Dawling accepted as a gentleman the event his evening paper had proclaimed; in view of which I snatched a moment to nudge him a hint that he might offer Mrs. Meldrum his hand. He returned me a heavy head-shake, and I judged that marriage would henceforth strike him very much as the traffic of the street may strike some poor incurable at the window of an hospital. Circumstances arising at this time led to my making an absence from England, and circumstances already existing offered him a firm basis for similar action. He had after all the usual resource of a Briton—he could take to his boats, always drawn up in our background. He started on a journey round the globe, and I was left with nothing but my inference as to what might have happened. Later observation however only confirmed my belief that if at any time during the couple of months after Flora Saunt's brilliant engagement he had made up, as they say, to the good lady of Folkestone, that good lady would not have pushed him over the cliff. Strange as she was to behold I knew of cases in which she had been obliged to administer that shove. I went to New York to paint a couple of portraits; but I found, once on the spot, that I had counted without Chicago, where I was invited to blot out this harsh discrimination by the production of some dozen. I spent a year in America and should probably have spent a second had I not been summoned back to England by alarming news from my mother. Her strength had failed, and as soon as I reached London I hurried down to Folkestone, arriving just at the moment to offer a welcome to some slight symptom of a rally. She had been much worse but was now a little better; and though I found nothing but satisfaction in having come to her I saw after a few hours that my London studio, where arrears of work had already met me, would be my place to await whatever might next occur. Yet before returning to town I called on Mrs. Meldrum, from whom I had not had a line, and my view of whom, with the adjacent objects, as I had left them, had been intercepted by a luxuriant foreground.

Before I had gained her house I met her, as I supposed, coming toward me across the down, greeting me from afar with the familiar twinkle of her great vitreous badge; and as it was late in the autumn and the esplanade a blank I was free to acknowledge this signal by cutting a caper on the grass. My enthusiasm dropped indeed the next moment, for I had seen in a few more seconds that the person thus assaulted had by no means the figure of my military friend. I felt a shock much greater than any I should have thought possible when on this person's drawing near I knew her for poor little Flora Saunt. At what moment she had recognised me belonged to an order of mysteries over which, it quickly came home to me, one would never linger again: once we were face to face it so chiefly mattered that I should succeed in looking entirely unastonished. All I at first saw was the big gold bar crossing each of her lenses, over which something convex and grotesque, like the eyes of a large insect, something that now represented her whole personality seemed, as out of the orifice of a prison, to strain forward and press. The face had shrunk away: it looked smaller, appeared even to look plain; it was at all events, so far as the effect on a spectator was concerned, wholly sacrificed to this huge apparatus of sight. There was no smile in it, and she made no motion to take my offered hand.

"I had no idea you were down here!" I said and I wondered whether she didn't know me at all or knew me only by my voice.

"You thought I was Mrs. Meldrum," she ever so quietly answered.

It was just this low pitch that made me protest with laughter. "Oh yes, you have a tremendous deal in common with Mrs. Meldrum! I've just returned to England after a long absence and I'm on my way to see her. Won't you come with me?" It struck me that her old reason for keeping clear of our friend was well disposed of now.

"I've just left her. I'm staying with her." She stood solemnly fixing me with her goggles. "Would you like to paint me now?" she asked. She seemed to speak, with intense gravity, from behind a mask or a cage.

There was nothing to do but treat the question still with high spirits. "It would be a fascinating little artistic problem!" That something was wrong it wasn't difficult to see, but a good deal more than met the eye might be presumed to be wrong if Flora was under Mrs. Meldrum's roof. I hadn't for a year had much time to think of her, but my imagination had had ground for lodging her in more gilded halls. One of the last things I had heard before leaving England was that in commemoration of the new relationship she had gone to stay with Lady Considine. This had made me take everything else for granted, and the noisy American world had deafened my care to possible contradictions. Her spectacles were at present a direct contradiction; they seemed a negation not only of new relationships but of every old one as well. I remember nevertheless that when after a moment she walked beside me on the grass I found myself nervously hoping she wouldn't as yet at any rate tell me anything very dreadful; so that to stave off this danger I harried her with questions about Mrs. Meldrum and, without waiting for replies, became profuse on the subject of my own doings. My companion was finely silent, and I felt both as if she were watching my nervousness with a sort of sinister irony and as if I were talking to some different and strange person. Flora plain and obscure and dumb was no Flora at all. At Mrs. Meldrum's door she turned off with the observation that as there was certainly a great deal I should have to say to our friend she had better not go in with me. I looked at her again—I had been keeping my eyes away from her—but only to meet her magnified stare. I greatly desired in truth to see Mrs. Meldrum alone, but there was something so grim in the girl's trouble that I hesitated to fall in with this idea of dropping her. Yet one couldn't express a compassion without seeming to take for granted more trouble than there actually might have been. I reflected that I must really figure to her as a fool, which was an entertainment I had never expected to give her. It rolled over me there for the first time—it has come back to me since—that there is, wondrously, in very deep and even in very foolish misfortune a dignity still finer than in the most inveterate habit of being all right. I couldn't have to her the manner of treating it as a mere detail that I was face to face with a part of what, at our last meeting, we had had such a scene about; but while I was trying to think of some manner that I *could* have she said quite colourlessly, though somehow as if she might never see me again: "Good-bye. I'm going to take my walk."

"All alone?"

She looked round the great bleak cliff-top. "With whom should I go? Besides I like to be alone—for the present."

This gave me the glimmer of a vision that she regarded her disfigurement as temporary, and the confidence came to me that she would never, for her happiness, cease to be a creature of illusions. It enabled me to exclaim, smiling brightly and feeling indeed idiotic: "Oh I shall see you again! But I hope you'll have a very pleasant walk."

"All my walks are pleasant, thank you—they do me such a lot of good." She was as quiet as a mouse, and her words seemed to me stupendous in their wisdom. "I take several a day," she continued. She might have been an ancient woman responding with humility at the church door to the patronage of the parson. "The more I take the better I feel. I'm ordered by the doctors to keep all the while in the air and go in for plenty of exercise. It keeps up my general health, you know, and if that goes on improving as it has lately done everything will soon be all right. All that was the matter with me before—and always; it was too reckless!—was that I neglected my general health. It acts directly on the state of the particular organ. So I'm going three miles."

I grinned at her from the doorstep while Mrs. Meldrum's maid stood there to admit me. "Oh I'm so glad," I said, looking at her as she paced away with the pretty flutter she had kept and remembering the day when, while she rejoined Lord Iffield, I had indulged in the same observation. Her air of assurance was on this occasion not less than it had been on that; but I recalled that she had then struck me as marching off to her doom. Was she really now marching away from it?

CHAPTER XI

As soon as I saw Mrs. Meldrum I of course broke out. "Is there anything in it? *Is* her general health—?"

Mrs. Meldrum checked me with her great amused blare. "You've already seen her and she has told you her wondrous tale? What's 'in it' is what has been in everything she has ever done—the most comical, tragical belief in herself. She thinks she's doing a 'cure.'"

"And what does her husband think?"

"Her husband? What husband?"

"Hasn't she then married Lord Iffield?"

"Vous-en-êtes là?" cried my hostess. "Why he behaved like a regular beast."

"How should I know? You never wrote me." Mrs. Meldrum hesitated, covering me with what poor Flora called the particular organ. "No, I didn't write you—I abstained on purpose. If I kept quiet I thought you mightn't hear over there what had happened. If you should hear I was afraid you would stir up Mr. Dawling."

"Stir him up?"

"Urge him to fly to the rescue; write out to him that there was another chance for him."

"I wouldn't have done it," I said.

"Well," Mrs. Meldrum replied, "it was not my business to give you an opportunity."

"In short you were afraid of it."

Again she hesitated and though it may have been only my fancy I thought she considerably reddened. At all events she laughed out. Then "I was afraid of it!" she very honestly answered.

"But doesn't he know? Has he given no sign?"

"Every sign in life—he came straight back to her. He did everything to get her to listen to him, but she hasn't the smallest idea of it."

"Has he seen her as she is now?" I presently and just a trifle awkwardly enquired.

"Indeed he has, and borne it like a hero. He told me all about it."

"How much you've all been through!" I found occasion to remark. "Then what has become of him?"

"He's at home in Hampshire. He has got back his old place and I believe by this time his old sisters. It's not half a bad little place."

"Yet its attractions say nothing to Flora?"

"Oh Flora's by no means on her back!" my fried declared.

"She's not on her back because she's on yours. Have you got her for the rest of your life?"

Once more Mrs. Meldrum genially glared. "Did she tell you how much the Hammond Synges have kindly left her to live on? Not quite eighty pounds a year."

"That's a good deal, but it won't pay the oculist. What was it that at last induced her to submit to him?"

"Her general collapse after that brute of an Iffield's rupture. She cried her eyes out—she passed through a horror of black darkness. Then came a gleam of light, and the light appears to have broadened. She went into goggles as repentant Magdalens go into the Catholic church."

"In spite of which you don't think she'll be saved?"

"*She* thinks she will—that's all I can tell you. There's no doubt that when once she brought herself to accept her real remedy, as she calls it, she began to enjoy a relief that she had never known. That feeling, very new and in spite of what she pays for it most refreshing, has given her something to hold on by, begotten in her foolish little mind a belief that, as she says, she's on the mend and that in the course of time, if she leads a tremendously healthy life, she'll be able to take off her muzzle and become as dangerous again as ever. It keeps her going."

"And what keeps you? You're good until the parties begin again."

"Oh she doesn't object to me now!" smiled Mrs. Meldrum. "I'm going to take her abroad; we shall be a pretty pair." I was struck with this energy and after a moment I enquired the reason of it. "It's to divert her mind," my friend replied, reddening again a little, I thought. "We shall go next week: I've only waited to see how your mother would be before starting." I expressed to her hereupon my sense of her extraordinary merit and also that of the inconceivability of Flora's fancying herself still in a situation not to jump at the chance of marrying a man like Dawling. "She says he's too ugly; she says he's too dreary; she says in fact he's 'nobody,'" Mrs. Meldrum pursued. "She says above all that he's not 'her own sort.' She doesn't deny that he's good, but she finds him impossibly ridiculous. He's quite the last person she would ever dream of." I was almost disposed on hearing this to protest that if the girl had so little proper feeling her noble suitor had perhaps served her right; but after a while my curiosity as to just how her noble suitor *had* served her got the better of that emotion, and I asked a question or two which led my companion again to apply to him the invidious term I have already quoted. What had happened was simply that Flora had at the eleventh hour broken down in the attempt to put him off with an uncandid account of her infirmity and that his lordship's interest in her had not been proof against the discovery of the way she had practised on him. Her dissimulation, he was obliged to perceive, had been infernally deep. The future in short assumed a new complexion for him when looked at through the grim glasses of a bride who, as he had said to some one, couldn't really, when you came to find out, see her hand before her face. He had conducted himself like any other jockeyed customer—he had returned the animal as unsound. He had backed out in his own way, giving the business, by some sharp shuffle, such a turn as to make the rupture ostensibly Flora's, but he had none the less remorselessly and basely backed out. He had cared for her lovely face, cared for it in the amused and haunted way it had been her poor little delusive gift to make men care; and her lovely face, damn it, with the monstrous gear she had begun to rig upon it, was just what had let him in. He had in the judgment of his family done everything that could be expected of him; he had made— Mrs. Meldrum had herself seen the letter—a "handsome" offer of pecuniary compensation. Oh if Flora, with her incredible buoyancy, was in a manner on her feet again now it was not that she had not for weeks and weeks been prone in the dust. Strange were the humiliations, the forms of anguish, it was given some natures to survive. That Flora had survived was perhaps after all a proof she was reserved for some final mercy. "But she has been in the abysses at any rate," said Mrs. Meldrum, "and I really don't think I can tell you what pulled her through."

"I think I can tell *you*," I returned. "What in the world but Mrs. Meldrum?"

At the end of an hour Flora had not come in, and I was obliged to announce that I should have but time to reach the station, where I was to find my luggage in charge of my mother's servant. Mrs. Meldrum put before me the question of waiting till a later train, so as not to lose our young lady, but I confess I gave this alternative a consideration less acute than I pretended. Somehow I didn't care if I did lose our young lady. Now that I knew the worst that had befallen her it struck me still less as possible to meet her on the ground of condolence; and with the sad appearance she wore to me what other ground was left? I lost her, but I caught my train. In truth she was so changed that one hated to see it; and now that she was in charitable hands one didn't feel compelled to make great efforts. I had studied her face for a particular beauty; I had lived with that beauty and reproduced it; but I knew what belonged to my trade well enough to be sure it was gone for ever.

CHAPTER XII

I was soon called back to Folkestone; but Mrs. Meldrum and her young friend had already left England, finding to that end every convenience on the spot and not having had to come up to town. My thoughts however were so painfully engaged there that I should in any case have had little attention for them: the event occurred that was to bring my series of visits to a close. When this high tide had ebbed I returned to America and to my interrupted work, which had opened out on such a scale that, with a deep plunge into a great chance, I was three good years in rising again to the surface. There are nymphs and naiads moreover in the American depths: they may have had something to do with the duration of my dive. I mention them to account for a grave misdemeanor—the fact that after the first year I rudely neglected Mrs. Meldrum. She had written to me from Florence after my mother's death and had mentioned in a postscript that in our young lady's calculations the lowest figures were now Italian counts. This was a good omen, and if in subsequent letters there was no news of a sequel I was content to accept small things and to believe that grave tidings, should there be any, would come to me in due course. The gravity of what might happen to a featherweight became indeed with time and distance less appreciable, and I was not without an impression that Mrs. Meldrum, whose sense of proportion was not the least of her merits, had no idea of boring the world with the ups and downs of her pensioner. The poor girl grew dusky and dim, a small fitful memory, a regret tempered by the comfortable consciousness of how kind Mrs. Meldrum would always be to her. I was professionally more preoccupied than I had ever been, and I had swarms of pretty faces in my eyes and a chorus of loud tones in my ears. Geoffrey Dawling had on his return to England written me two or three letters: his last information had been that he was going into the figures of rural illiteracy. I was delighted to receive it and had no doubt that if he should go into figures they would, as they are said to be able to prove anything, prove at least that my advice was sound and that he had wasted time enough. This quickened on my part another hope, a hope suggested by some roundabout rumour—I forget how it reached me—that he was engaged to a girl down in Hampshire. He turned out not to be, but I felt sure that if only he went into figures deep enough he would become, among the girls down in Hampshire or elsewhere, one of those numerous prizes of battle whose defences are practically not on the scale of their provocations. I nursed in short the thought that it was probably open to him to develop as one of the types about whom, as the years go on, superficial critics wonder without relief how they ever succeeded in dragging a bride to the altar. He never alluded to Flora Saunt; and there was in his silence about her, quite as in Mrs. Meldrum's, an element of instinctive tact, a brief implication that if you didn't happen to have been in love with her there was nothing to be said.

Within a week after my return to London I went to the opera, of which I had always been much of a devotee. I arrived too late for the first act of "Lohengrin," but the second was just beginning, and I gave myself up to it with no more than a glance at the house. When it was over I treated myself, with my glass, from my place in the stalls, to a general survey of the boxes, making doubtless on their contents the reflections, pointed by comparison, that are most familiar to the wanderer restored to London. There was the common sprinkling of pretty women, but I suddenly noted that one of these was far prettier than the others. This lady, alone in one of the smaller receptacles of the grand tier and already the aim of fifty tentative glasses, which she sustained with admirable serenity, this single exquisite figure, placed in the quarter furthest removed from my stall, was a person, I immediately felt, to cause one's curiosity to linger. Dressed in white, with diamonds in her hair and pearls on her neck, she had a pale radiance of beauty which even at that distance made her a distinguished presence and, with the air that easily attaches to lonely loveliness in public places, an agreeable mystery. A mystery however she remained to me only for a minute after I had levelled my glass at her: I feel to this moment the startled thrill, the shock almost of joy, with which I translated her vague brightness into a resurrection of Flora. I say a resurrection, because, to put it crudely, I had on that last occasion left our young woman for dead. At present perfectly alive again, she was altered only, as it were, by this fact of life. A little older, a little quieter, a little finer and a good deal fairer, she was simply transfigured by having recovered. Sustained by the reflection that even her recovery wouldn't enable her to distinguish me in the crowd, I was free to look at her well. Then it was it came home to me that my vision of her in her great goggles had been cruelly final. As her beauty was all there was of her, that machinery had extinguished her, and so far as I had thought of her in the interval I had thought of her as buried in the tomb her stern specialist had built. With the sense that she had escaped from it came a lively wish to return to her; and if I didn't straightway leave my place and rush round the theatre and up to her box it was because I was fixed to the spot some moments longer by the simple inability to cease looking at her.

She had been from the first of my seeing her practically motionless, leaning back in her chair with a kind of thoughtful grace and with her eyes vaguely directed, as it seemed on me, to one of the boxes on my side of the house and consequently over my head and out of my sight. The only movement she made for some time was to finger with an ungloved hand and as if with the habit of fondness the row of pearls on her neck, which my glass showed me to be large and splendid. Her diamonds and pearls, in her solitude, mystified me, making me, as she had had no such brave jewels in the days of the Hammond Synges, wonder what undreamt-of improvement had taken place in her fortunes. The ghost of a question hovered there a moment: could anything so prodigious have happened as that on her tested and proved amendment Lord Iffield had taken her back? This could scarce have without my hearing of it; and moreover if she had become a person of such fashion where was the little court one would naturally see at her elbow? Her isolation was puzzling, though it could easily suggest that she was but momentarily alone. If she had come with Mrs. Meldrum that lady would have taken advantage of the interval to pay a visit to some other box—doubtless the box at which Flora had just been looking. Mrs. Meldrum didn't account for the jewels, but the revival of Flora's beauty accounted for anything. She presently moved her eyes over the house, and I felt them brush me again like the wings of a dove. I don't know what quick pleasure flickered into the hope that she would at last see me. She did see me: she suddenly bent forward to take up the little double-barrelled ivory glass that rested on the edge of the box and to all appearance fix me with it. I smiled from my place straight up at the searching lenses, and after an instant she dropped them and smiled as straight back at me. Oh her smile—it was her old smile, her young smile, her very own smile made perfect! I instantly left my stall and hurried off for a nearer view of it; quite flushed, I remember, as I went with the annoyance of having happened to think of the idiotic way I had tried to paint her. Poor Iffield with his sample of that error, and still poorer Dawling in particular with *his*! I hadn't touched her, I was professionally humiliated, and as the attendant in the lobby opened her box for me I felt that the very first thing I should have to say to her would be that she must absolutely sit to me again.

CHAPTER XIII

She gave me the smile once more as over her shoulder, from her chair, she turned her face to me. "Here you are again!" she exclaimed with her disgloved hand put up a little backward for me to take. I dropped into a chair just behind her and, having taken it and noted that one of the curtains of the box would make the demonstration sufficiently private, bent my lips over it and impressed them on its finger-tips. It was given me however, to my astonishment, to feel next that all the privacy in the world couldn't have sufficed to mitigate the start with which she greeted this free application of my moustache: the blood had jumped to her face, she quickly recovered her hand and jerked at me, twisting herself round, a vacant challenging stare. During the next few instants several extraordinary things happened, the first of which was that now I was close to them the eyes of loveliness I had come up to look into didn't show at all the conscious light I had just been pleased to see them flash across the house: they showed on the contrary, to my confusion, a strange sweet blankness, an expression I failed to give a meaning to until, without delay, I felt on my arm, directed to it as if instantly to efface the effect of her start, the grasp of the hand she had impulsively snatched from me. It was the irrepressible question in this grasp that stopped on my lips all sound of salutation. She had mistaken my entrance for that of another person, a pair of lips without a moustache. She was feeling me to see who I was! With the perception of this and of her not seeing me I sat gaping at her and at the wild word that didn't come, the right word to express or to disguise my dismay. What was the right word to commemorate one's sudden discovery, at the very moment too at which one had been most encouraged to count on better things, that one's dear old friend had gone blind? Before the answer to this question dropped upon me—and the moving moments, though few, seemed many—I heard, with the sound of voices, the click of the attendant's key on the other side of the door. Poor Flora heard also and on hearing, still with her hand on my arm, brightened again as I had a minute since seen her brighten across the house: she had the sense of the return of the person she

had taken me for—the person with the right pair of lips, as to whom I wa
for that matter much more in the dark than she. I gasped, but my word
had come: if she had lost her sight it was in this very loss that she had found
again her beauty. I managed to speak while we were still alone, before her
companion had appeared. "You're lovelier at this day than you have ever
been in your life!" At the sound of my voice and that of the opening of the
door her impatience broke into audible joy. She sprang up, recognising me
always holding me, and gleefully cried to a gentleman who was arrested in
the doorway by the sight of me: "He has come back, he has come back, and
you should have heard what he says of me!" The gentleman was Geoffrey
Dawling, and I thought it best to let him hear on the spot. "How beautiful
she is, my dear man—but how extraordinarily beautiful! More beautiful at
this hour than ever, ever before!"

It gave them almost equal pleasure and made Dawling blush to his eyes;
while this in turn produced, in spite of deepened astonishment, a blest snap
of the strain I had been struggling with. I wanted to embrace them both,
and while the opening bars of another scene rose from the orchestra I almost
did embrace Dawling, whose first emotion on beholding me had visibly and
ever so oddly been a consciousness of guilt. I had caught him somehow in
the act, though that was as yet all I knew; but by the time we sank noiselessly
into our chairs again—for the music was supreme, Wagner passed first—my
demonstration ought pretty well to have given him the limit of the criticism
he had to fear. I myself indeed, while the opera blazed, was only too afraid
he might divine in our silent closeness the very moral of my optimism, which
was simply the comfort I had gathered from seeing that if our companion's
beauty lived again her vanity partook of its life. I had hit on the right note—
that was what eased me off: it drew all pain for the next half-hour from the
sense of the deep darkness in which the stricken woman sat. If the music, in
that darkness, happily soared and swelled for her, it beat its wings in unison
with those of a gratified passion. A great deal came and went between us
without profaning the occasion, so that I could feel at the end of twenty
minutes as if I knew almost everything he might in kindness have to tell me;
knew even why Flora, while I stared at her from the stalls, had misled me
by the use of ivory and crystal and by appearing to recognise me and smile.

She leaned back in her chair in luxurious ease: I had from the first become aware that the way she fingered her pearls was a sharp image of the wedded state. Nothing of old had seemed wanting to her assurance, but I hadn't then dreamed of the art with which she would wear that assurance as a married woman. She had taken him when everything had failed; he had taken her when she herself had done so. His embarrassed eyes confessed it all, confessed the deep peace he found in it. They only didn't tell me why he had not written to me, nor clear up as yet a minor obscurity. Flora after a while again lifted the glass from the ledge of the box and elegantly swept the house with it. Then, by the mere instinct of her grace, a motion but half conscious, she inclined her head into the void with the sketch of a salute, producing, I could see, a perfect imitation of response to some homage. Dawling and I looked at each other again; the tears came into his eyes. She was playing at perfection still, and her misfortune only simplified the process.

I recognised that this was as near as I should ever come, certainly as I should come that night, to pressing on her misfortune. Neither of us would name it more than we were doing then, and Flora would never name it at all. Little by little I saw that what had occurred was, strange as it might appear, the best thing for her happiness. The question was now only of her beauty and her being seen and marvelled at; with Dawling to do for her everything in life her activity was limited to that. Such an activity was all within her scope; it asked nothing of her that she couldn't splendidly give. As from time to time in our delicate communion she turned her face to me with the parody of a look I lost none of the signs of its strange new glory. The expression of the eyes was a rub of pastel from a master's thumb; the whole head, stamped with a sort of showy suffering, had gained a fineness from what she had passed through. Yes, Flora was settled for life—nothing could hurt her further. I foresaw the particular praise she would mostly incur—she would be invariably "interesting." She would charm with her pathos more even than she had charmed with her pleasure. For herself above all she was fixed for ever, rescued from all change and ransomed from all doubt. Her old certainties, her old vanities were justified and sanctified, and in the darkness that had closed upon her one object remained clear. That object, as unfading as a mosaic mask, was fortunately the loveliest she could possibly look upon.

The greatest blessing of all was of course that Dawling thought so. Her future was ruled with the straightest line, and so for that matter was his. There were two facts to which before I left my friends I gave time to sink into my spirit. One was that he had changed by some process as effective as Flora's change, had been simplified somehow into service as she had been simplified into success. He was such a picture of inspired intervention as I had never yet conceived: he would exist henceforth for the sole purpose of rendering unnecessary, or rather impossible, any reference even on her own part to his wife's infirmity. Oh yes, how little desire he would ever give *me* to refer to it! He principally after a while made me feel—and this was my second lesson—that, good-natured as he was, my being there to see it all oppressed him; so that by the time the act ended I recognised that I too had filled out my hour. Dawling remembered things; I think he caught in my very face the irony of old judgments: they made him thresh about in his chair. I said to Flora as I took leave of her that I would come to see her, but I may mention that I never went. I'd go to-morrow if I hear she wants me; but what in the world can she ever want? As I quitted them I laid my hand on Dawling's arm, and drew him for a moment into the lobby.

"Why did you never write to me of your marriage?"

He smiled uncomfortably, showing his long yellow teeth and something more. "I don't know—the whole thing gave me such a tremendous lot to do."

This was the first dishonest speech I had heard him make: he really hadn't written because an idea that I would think him a still bigger fool than before. I didn't insist, but I tried there in the lobby, so far as a pressure of his hand could serve me, to give him a notion of what I thought him. "I can't at any rate make out," I said, "why I didn't hear from Mrs. Meldrum."

"She didn't write to you?"

"Never a word. What has become of her?"

"I think she's at Folkestone," Dawling returned; "but I'm sorry to say that practically she has ceased to see us."

"You haven't quarrelled with her?"

"How *could* we? Think of all we owe her. At the time of our marriage, and for months before, she did everything for us: I don't know how we should have managed without her. But since then she has never been near us and has given us rather markedly little encouragement to keep up relations with her."

I was struck with this, though of course I admit I am struck with all sorts of things. "Well," I said after a moment, "even if I could imagine a reason for that attitude it wouldn't explain why she shouldn't have taken account of my natural interest."

"Just so." Dawling's face was a windowless wall. He could contribute nothing to the mystery and, quitting him, I carried it away. It was not till I went down to ace Mrs. Meldrum that was really dispelled. She didn't want to hear of them or to talk of them, not a bit, and it was just in the same spirit that she hadn't wanted to write of them. She had done everything in the world for them, but now, thank heaven, the hard business was over. After I had taken this in, which I was quick to do, we quite avoided the subject. She simply couldn't bear it.

About Author

Henry James OM (15 April 1843 – 28 February 1916) was an American-British author regarded as a key transitional figure between literary realism and literary modernism, and is considered by many to be among the greatest novelists in the English language. He was the son of Henry James Sr. and the brother of renowned philosopher and psychologist William James and diarist Alice James.

He is best known for a number of novels dealing with the social and marital interplay between émigré Americans, English people, and continental Europeans. Examples of such novels include The Portrait of a Lady, The Ambassadors, and The Wings of the Dove. His later works were increasingly experimental. In describing the internal states of mind and social dynamics of his characters, James often made use of a style in which ambiguous or contradictory motives and impressions were overlaid or juxtaposed in the discussion of a character's psyche. For their unique ambiguity, as well as for other aspects of their composition, his late works have been compared to impressionist painting.

His novella The Turn of the Screw has garnered a reputation as the most analysed and ambiguous ghost story in the English language and remains his most widely adapted work in other media. He also wrote a number of other highly regarded ghost stories and is considered one of the greatest masters of the field.

James published articles and books of criticism, travel, biography, autobiography, and plays. Born in the United States, James largely relocated to Europe as a young man and eventually settled in England, becoming a British subject in 1915, one year before his death. James was nominated for the Nobel Prize in Literature in 1911, 1912 and 1916.

Life

Early years, 1843–1883

James was born at 2 Washington Place in New York City on 15 April 1843. His parents were Mary Walsh and Henry James Sr. His father was intelligent and steadfastly congenial. He was a lecturer and philosopher who had inherited independent means from his father, an Albany banker and investor. Mary came from a wealthy family long settled in New York City. Her sister Katherine lived with her adult family for an extended period of time. Henry Jr. had three brothers, William, who was one year his senior, and younger brothers Wilkinson (Wilkie) and Robertson. His younger sister was Alice. Both of his parents were of Irish and Scottish descent.

The family first lived in Albany, at 70 N. Pearl St., and then moved to Fourteenth Street in New York City when James was still a young boy. His education was calculated by his father to expose him to many influences, primarily scientific and philosophical; it was described by Percy Lubbock, the editor of his selected letters, as "extraordinarily haphazard and promiscuous." James did not share the usual education in Latin and Greek classics. Between 1855 and 1860, the James' household traveled to London, Paris, Geneva, Boulogne-sur-Mer and Newport, Rhode Island, according to the father's current interests and publishing ventures, retreating to the United States when funds were low. Henry studied primarily with tutors and briefly attended schools while the family traveled in Europe. Their longest stays were in France, where Henry began to feel at home and became fluent in French. He was afflicted with a stutter, which seems to have manifested itself only when he spoke English; in French, he did not stutter.

In 1860 the family returned to Newport. There Henry became a friend of the painter John La Farge, who introduced him to French literature, and in particular, to Balzac. James later called Balzac his "greatest master," and said that he had learned more about the craft of fiction from him than from anyone else.

In the autumn of 1861 Henry received an injury, probably to his back, while fighting a fire. This injury, which resurfaced at times throughout his life, made him unfit for military service in the American Civil War.

In 1864 the James family moved to Boston, Massachusetts to be near William, who had enrolled first in the Lawrence Scientific School at Harvard and then in the medical school. In 1862 Henry attended Harvard Law School, but realised that he was not interested in studying law. He pursued his interest in literature and associated with authors and critics William Dean Howells and Charles Eliot Norton in Boston and Cambridge, formed lifelong friendships with Oliver Wendell Holmes Jr., the future Supreme Court Justice, and with James and Annie Fields, his first professional mentors.

His first published work was a review of a stage performance, "Miss Maggie Mitchell in Fanchon the Cricket," published in 1863. About a year later, A Tragedy of Error, his first short story, was published anonymously. James's first payment was for an appreciation of Sir Walter Scott's novels, written for the North American Review. He wrote fiction and non-fiction pieces for The Nation and Atlantic Monthly, where Fields was editor. In 1871 he published his first novel, Watch and Ward, in serial form in the Atlantic Monthly. The novel was later published in book form in 1878.

During a 14-month trip through Europe in 1869–70 he met Ruskin, Dickens, Matthew Arnold, William Morris, and George Eliot. Rome impressed him profoundly. "Here I am then in the Eternal City," he wrote to his brother William. "At last—for the first time—I live!" He attempted to support himself as a freelance writer in Rome, then secured a position as Paris correspondent for the New York Tribune, through the influence of its editor John Hay. When these efforts failed he returned to New York City. During 1874 and 1875 he published Transatlantic Sketches, A Passionate Pilgrim, and Roderick Hudson. During this early period in his career he was influenced by Nathaniel Hawthorne.

In 1869 he settled in London. There he established relationships with Macmillan and other publishers, who paid for serial installments that they would later publish in book form. The audience for these serialized novels was largely made up of middle-class women, and James struggled to fashion serious literary work within the strictures imposed by editors' and publishers' notions of what was suitable for young women to read. He lived in rented rooms but was able to join gentlemen's clubs that had libraries and where he could entertain male friends. He was introduced to English society by Henry Adams and Charles Milnes Gaskell, the latter introducing him to the Travellers' and the Reform Clubs.

In the fall of 1875 he moved to the Latin Quarter of Paris. Aside from two trips to America, he spent the next three decades—the rest of his life—in Europe. In Paris he met Zola, Alphonse Daudet, Maupassant, Turgenev, and others. He stayed in Paris only a year before moving to London.

In England he met the leading figures of politics and culture. He continued to be a prolific writer, producing The American (1877), The Europeans (1878), a revision of Watch and Ward (1878), French Poets and Novelists (1878), Hawthorne (1879), and several shorter works of fiction. In 1878 Daisy Miller established his fame on both sides of the Atlantic. It drew notice perhaps mostly because it depicted a woman whose behavior is outside the social norms of Europe. He also began his first masterpiece, The Portrait of a Lady, which would appear in 1881.

In 1877 he first visited Wenlock Abbey in Shropshire, home of his friend Charles Milnes Gaskell whom he had met through Henry Adams. He was much inspired by the darkly romantic Abbey and the surrounding countryside, which features in his essay Abbeys and Castles. In particular the gloomy monastic fishponds behind the Abbey are said to have inspired the lake in The Turn of the Screw.

While living in London, James continued to follow the careers of the "French realists", Émile Zola in particular. Their stylistic methods influenced his own work in the years to come. Hawthorne's influence on him faded during this period, replaced by George Eliot and Ivan Turgenev. 1879–1882 saw the publication of The Europeans, Washington Square, Confidence, and The Portrait of a Lady. He visited America in 1882–1883, then returned to London.

The period from 1881 to 1883 was marked by several losses. His mother died in 1881, followed by his father a few months later, and then by his brother Wilkie. Emerson, an old family friend, died in 1882. His friend Turgenev died in 1883.

Middle years, 1884–1897

In 1884 James made another visit to Paris. There he met again with Zola, Daudet, and Goncourt. He had been following the careers of the French "realist" or "naturalist" writers, and was increasingly influenced by them. In 1886, he published The Bostonians and The Princess Casamassima, both influenced by the French writers he'd studied assiduously. Critical reaction and sales were poor. He wrote to Howells that the books had hurt his career rather than helped because they had "reduced the desire, and demand, for my productions to zero". During this time he became friends with Robert Louis Stevenson, John Singer Sargent, Edmund Gosse, George du Maurier, Paul Bourget, and Constance Fenimore Woolson. His third novel from the 1880s was The Tragic Muse. Although he was following the precepts of Zola in his novels of the '80s, their tone and attitude are closer to the fiction of Alphonse Daudet. The lack of critical and financial success for his novels during this period led him to try writing for the theatre. (His dramatic works and his experiences with theatre are discussed below.)

In the last quarter of 1889, he started translating "for pure and copious lucre" Port Tarascon, the third volume of Alphonse Daudet adventures of Tartarin de Tarascon. Serialized in Harper's Monthly Magazine from June 1890, this translation praised as "clever" by The Spectator was published in January 1891 by Sampson Low, Marston, Searle & Rivington.

After the stage failure of Guy Domville in 1895, James was near despair and thoughts of death plagued him. The years spent on dramatic works were not entirely a loss. As he moved into the last phase of his career he found ways to adapt dramatic techniques into the novel form.

In the late 1880s and throughout the 1890s James made several trips through Europe. He spent a long stay in Italy in 1887. In that year the short novel The Aspern Papers and The Reverberator were published.

Late years, 1898–1916

In 1897–1898 he moved to Rye, Sussex, and wrote The Turn of the Screw. 1899–1900 saw the publication of The Awkward Age and The Sacred

Fount. During 1902–1904 he wrote The Ambassadors, The Wings of the Dove, and The Golden Bowl.

In 1904 he revisited America and lectured on Balzac. In 1906–1910 he published The American Scene and edited the "New York Edition", a 24-volume collection of his works. In 1910 his brother William died; Henry had just joined William from an unsuccessful search for relief in Europe on what then turned out to be his (Henry's) last visit to the United States (from summer 1910 to July 1911), and was near him, according to a letter he wrote, when he died.

In 1913 he wrote his autobiographies, A Small Boy and Others, and Notes of a Son and Brother. After the outbreak of the First World War in 1914 he did war work. In 1915 he became a British subject and was awarded the Order of Merit the following year. He died on 28 February 1916, in Chelsea, London. As he requested, his ashes were buried in Cambridge Cemetery in Massachusetts.

Biographers

James regularly rejected suggestions that he should marry, and after settling in London proclaimed himself "a bachelor". F. W. Dupee, in several volumes on the James family, originated the theory that he had been in love with his cousin Mary ("Minnie") Temple, but that a neurotic fear of sex kept him from admitting such affections: "James's invalidism ... was itself the symptom of some fear of or scruple against sexual love on his part." Dupee used an episode from James's memoir A Small Boy and Others, recounting a dream of a Napoleonic image in the Louvre, to exemplify James's romanticism about Europe, a Napoleonic fantasy into which he fled.

Dupee had not had access to the James family papers and worked principally from James's published memoir of his older brother, William, and the limited collection of letters edited by Percy Lubbock, heavily weighted toward James's last years. His account therefore moved directly from James's childhood, when he trailed after his older brother, to elderly invalidism. As more material became available to scholars, including the diaries of contemporaries and hundreds of affectionate and sometimes erotic letters written by James to younger men, the picture of neurotic celibacy gave way to a portrait of a closeted homosexual.

Between 1953 and 1972, Leon Edel authored a major five-volume biography of James, which accessed unpublished letters and documents after Edel gained the permission of James's family. Edel's portrayal of James included the suggestion he was celibate. It was a view first propounded by critic Saul Rosenzweig in 1943. In 1996 Sheldon M. Novick published Henry James: The Young Master, followed by Henry James: The Mature Master (2007). The first book "caused something of an uproar in Jamesian circles" as it challenged the previous received notion of celibacy, a once-familiar paradigm in biographies of homosexuals when direct evidence was non-existent. Novick also criticised Edel for following the discounted Freudian interpretation of homosexuality "as a kind of failure." The difference of opinion erupted in a series of exchanges between Edel and Novick which were published by the online magazine Slate, with the latter arguing that even the suggestion of celibacy went against James's own injunction "live!"—not "fantasize!"

A letter James wrote in old age to Hugh Walpole has been cited as an explicit statement of this. Walpole confessed to him of indulging in "high jinks", and James wrote a reply endorsing it: "We must know, as much as possible, in our beautiful art, yours & mine, what we are talking about — & the only way to know it is to have lived & loved & cursed & floundered & enjoyed & suffered — I don't think I regret a single 'excess' of my responsive youth".

The interpretation of James as living a less austere emotional life has been subsequently explored by other scholars. The often intense politics of Jamesian scholarship has also been the subject of studies. Author Colm Tóibín has said that Eve Kosofsky Sedgwick's Epistemology of the Closet made a landmark difference to Jamesian scholarship by arguing that he be read as a homosexual writer whose desire to keep his sexuality a secret shaped his layered style and dramatic artistry. According to Tóibín such a reading "removed James from the realm of dead white males who wrote about posh people. He became our contemporary."

James's letters to expatriate American sculptor Hendrik Christian Andersen have attracted particular attention. James met the 27-year-old Andersen in Rome in 1899, when James was 56, and wrote letters to Andersen that are intensely emotional: "I hold you, dearest boy, in my innermost love & count on your feeling me—in every throb of your soul". In a letter of 6 May 1904, to his brother William, James referred to himself as "always your hopelessly celibate even though sexagenarian Henry". How accurate that description might have been is the subject of contention among James's biographers, but the letters to Andersen were occasionally quasi-erotic: "I put, my dear boy, my arm around you, & feel the pulsation, thereby, as it were, of our excellent future & your admirable endowment." To his homosexual friend Howard Sturgis, James could write: "I repeat, almost to indiscretion, that I could live with you. Meanwhile I can only try to live without you."

His numerous letters to the many young gay men among his close male friends are more forthcoming. In a letter to Howard Sturgis, following a long visit, James refers jocularly to their "happy little congress of two" and in letters to Hugh Walpole he pursues convoluted jokes and puns about their relationship, referring to himself as an elephant who "paws you oh so benevolently" and winds about Walpole his "well meaning old trunk". His letters to Walter Berry printed by the Black Sun Press have long been celebrated for their lightly veiled eroticism.

He corresponded in almost equally extravagant language with his many female friends, writing, for example, to fellow novelist Lucy Clifford: "Dearest Lucy! What shall I say? when I love you so very, very much, and see you nine times for once that I see Others! Therefore I think that—if you want it made clear to the meanest intelligence—I love you more than I love Others." To his New York friend Mary Cadwalader Jones: "Dearest Mary Cadwalader. I yearn over you, but I yearn in vain; & your long silence really breaks my heart, mystifies, depresses, almost alarms me, to the point even of making me wonder if poor unconscious & doting old Célimare [Jones's pet name for James] has 'done' anything, in some dark somnambulism of the spirit, which has ... given you a bad moment, or a wrong impression, or a 'colourable pretext' ... However these things may be, he loves you as tenderly as ever;

nothing, to the end of time, will ever detach him from you, & he remembers those Eleventh St. matutinal intimes hours, those telephonic matinées, as the most romantic of his life ..." His long friendship with American novelist Constance Fenimore Woolson, in whose house he lived for a number of weeks in Italy in 1887, and his shock and grief over her suicide in 1894, are discussed in detail in Edel's biography and play a central role in a study by Lyndall Gordon. (Edel conjectured that Woolson was in love with James and killed herself in part because of his coldness, but Woolson's biographers have objected to Edel's account.)

Works

Style and themes

James is one of the major figures of trans-Atlantic literature. His works frequently juxtapose characters from the Old World (Europe), embodying a feudal civilisation that is beautiful, often corrupt, and alluring, and from the New World (United States), where people are often brash, open, and assertive and embody the virtues—freedom and a more highly evolved moral character—of the new American society. James explores this clash of personalities and cultures, in stories of personal relationships in which power is exercised well or badly. His protagonists were often young American women facing oppression or abuse, and as his secretary Theodora Bosanquet remarked in her monograph Henry James at Work:

> When he walked out of the refuge of his study and into the world and looked around him, he saw a place of torment, where creatures of prey perpetually thrust their claws into the quivering flesh of doomed, defenseless children of light ... His novels are a repeated exposure of this wickedness, a reiterated and passionate plea for the fullest freedom of development, unimperiled by reckless and barbarous stupidity.

Critics have jokingly described three phases in the development of James's prose: "James I, James II, and The Old Pretender." He wrote short stories and plays. Finally, in his third and last period he returned to the long, serialised novel. Beginning in the second period, but most noticeably in the third, he increasingly abandoned direct statement in favour of frequent double negatives, and complex descriptive imagery. Single paragraphs began to run for page after page, in which an initial noun would be succeeded by pronouns surrounded by clouds of adjectives and prepositional clauses, far from their original referents, and verbs would be deferred and then preceded by a series of adverbs. The overall effect could be a vivid evocation of a scene as perceived by a sensitive observer. It has been debated whether this change of style was engendered by James's shifting from writing to dictating to a typist, a change made during the composition of What Maisie Knew.

In its intense focus on the consciousness of his major characters, James's later work foreshadows extensive developments in 20th century fiction. Indeed, he might have influenced stream-of-consciousness writers such as Virginia Woolf, who not only read some of his novels but also wrote essays about them. Both contemporary and modern readers have found the late style difficult and unnecessary; his friend Edith Wharton, who admired him greatly, said that there were passages in his work that were all but incomprehensible. James was harshly portrayed by H. G. Wells as a hippopotamus laboriously attempting to pick up a pea that had got into a corner of its cage. The "late James" style was ably parodied by Max Beerbohm in "The Mote in the Middle Distance".

More important for his work overall may have been his position as an expatriate, and in other ways an outsider, living in Europe. While he came from middle-class and provincial beginnings (seen from the perspective of European polite society) he worked very hard to gain access to all levels of society, and the settings of his fiction range from working class to aristocratic, and often describe the efforts of middle-class Americans to make their way in European capitals. He confessed he got some of his best story ideas from gossip at the dinner table or at country house weekends. He worked for a living, however, and lacked the experiences of select schools, university, and army service, the common bonds of masculine society. He was furthermore a man whose tastes and interests were, according to the prevailing standards of Victorian era Anglo-American culture, rather feminine, and who was shadowed by the cloud of prejudice that then and later accompanied suspicions of his homosexuality. Edmund Wilson famously compared James's objectivity to Shakespeare's:

One would be in a position to appreciate James better if one compared him with the dramatists of the seventeenth century—Racine and Molière, whom he resembles in form as well as in point of view, and even Shakespeare, when allowances are made for the most extreme differences in subject and form. These poets are not, like Dickens and Hardy, writers of melodrama—either humorous or pessimistic, nor secretaries of society like Balzac, nor prophets like Tolstoy: they are occupied simply with the presentation of conflicts of moral character, which they do not concern themselves about softening or averting. They do not indict society for these situations: they regard them as universal and inevitable. They do not even blame God for allowing them: they accept them as the conditions of life.

It is also possible to see many of James's stories as psychological thought-experiments. In his preface to the New York edition of The American he describes the development of the story in his mind as exactly such: the "situation" of an American, "some robust but insidiously beguiled and betrayed, some cruelly wronged, compatriot..." with the focus of the story being on the response of this wronged man. The Portrait of a Lady may be an experiment to see what happens when an idealistic young woman suddenly becomes very rich. In many of his tales, characters seem to exemplify alternative futures and possibilities, as most markedly in "The Jolly Corner", in which the protagonist and a ghost-doppelganger live alternative American and European lives; and in others, like The Ambassadors, an older James seems fondly to regard his own younger self facing a crucial moment.

Major novels

The first period of James's fiction, usually considered to have culminated in The Portrait of a Lady, concentrated on the contrast between Europe and America. The style of these novels is generally straightforward and, though personally characteristic, well within the norms of 19th-century fiction. Roderick Hudson (1875) is a Künstlerroman that traces the development of the title character, an extremely talented sculptor. Although the book shows some signs of immaturity—this was James's first serious attempt at a full-length novel—it has attracted favourable comment due to the vivid realisation of the three major characters: Roderick Hudson, superbly gifted but unstable and unreliable; Rowland Mallet, Roderick's limited but much more mature friend and patron; and Christina Light, one of James's most enchanting and maddening femmes fatales. The pair of Hudson and Mallet has been seen as representing the two sides of James's own nature: the wildly imaginative artist and the brooding conscientious mentor.

In The Portrait of a Lady (1881) James concluded the first phase of his career with a novel that remains his most popular piece of long fiction. The story is of a spirited young American woman, Isabel Archer, who "affronts her destiny" and finds it overwhelming. She inherits a large amount of money and subsequently becomes the victim of Machiavellian scheming by two American expatriates. The narrative is set mainly in Europe, especially in England and Italy. Generally regarded as the masterpiece of his early phase, The Portrait of a Lady is described as a psychological novel, exploring the minds of his characters, and almost a work of social science, exploring the differences between Europeans and Americans, the old and the new worlds.

The second period of James's career, which extends from the publication of The Portrait of a Lady through the end of the nineteenth century, features less popular novels including The Princess Casamassima, published serially in The Atlantic Monthly in 1885–1886, and The Bostonians, published serially in The Century Magazine during the same period. This period also featured James's celebrated Gothic novella, The Turn of the Screw.

The third period of James's career reached its most significant achievement in three novels published just around the start of the 20th century: The Wings of the Dove (1902), The Ambassadors (1903), and The Golden Bowl (1904). Critic F. O. Matthiessen called this "trilogy" James's major phase, and these novels have certainly received intense critical study. It was the second-written of the books, The Wings of the Dove (1902) that was the first published because it attracted no serialization. This novel tells the story of Milly Theale, an American heiress stricken with a serious disease, and her impact on the people around her. Some of these people befriend Milly with honourable motives, while others are more self-interested. James stated in his autobiographical books that Milly was based on Minny Temple, his beloved cousin who died at an early age of tuberculosis. He said that he attempted in the novel to wrap her memory in the "beauty and dignity of art".

Shorter narratives

James was particularly interested in what he called the "beautiful and blest nouvelle", or the longer form of short narrative. Still, he produced a number of very short stories in which he achieved notable compression of sometimes complex subjects. The following narratives are representative of James's achievement in the shorter forms of fiction.

- "A Tragedy of Error" (1864), short story
- "The Story of a Year" (1865), short story
- A Passionate Pilgrim (1871), novella
- Madame de Mauves (1874), novella
- Daisy Miller (1878), novella
- The Aspern Papers (1888), novella
- The Lesson of the Master (1888), novella
- The Pupil (1891), short story
- "The Figure in the Carpet" (1896), short story
- The Beast in the Jungle (1903), novella
- An International Episode (1878)
- Picture and Text
- Four Meetings (1885)
- A London Life, and Other Tales (1889)
- The Spoils of Poynton (1896)

- Embarrassments (1896)

- The Two Magics: The Turn of the Screw, Covering End (1898)

- A Little Tour of France (1900)

- The Sacred Fount (1901)

- Views and Reviews (1908)

- The Wings of the Dove, Volume I (1902)

- The Wings of the Dove, Volume II (1909)

- The Finer Grain (1910)

- The Outcry (1911)

- Lady Barbarina: The Siege of London, An International Episode and Other Tales (1922)

- The Birthplace (1922)

Plays

At several points in his career James wrote plays, beginning with one-act plays written for periodicals in 1869 and 1871 and a dramatisation of his popular novella Daisy Miller in 1882. From 1890 to 1892, having received a bequest that freed him from magazine publication, he made a strenuous effort to succeed on the London stage, writing a half-dozen plays of which only one, a dramatisation of his novel The American, was produced. This play was performed for several years by a touring repertory company and had a respectable run in London, but did not earn very much money for James. His other plays written at this time were not produced.

In 1893, however, he responded to a request from actor-manager George Alexander for a serious play for the opening of his renovated St James's Theatre, and wrote a long drama, Guy Domville, which Alexander produced. There was a noisy uproar on the opening night, 5 January 1895 with hissing from the gallery when James took his bow after the final curtain and the author was upset. The play received moderately good reviews and had a modest run of four weeks before being taken off to make way for Oscar Wilde's The Importance of Being Earnest, which Alexander thought would have better prospects for the coming season.

After the stresses and disappointment of these efforts James insisted that he would write no more for the theatre, but within weeks had agreed to write a curtain-raiser for Ellen Terry. This became the one-act "Summersoft", which he later rewrote into a short story, "Covering End", and then expanded into a full-length play, The High Bid, which had a brief run in London in 1907, when James made another concerted effort to write for the stage. He wrote three new plays, two of which were in production when the death of Edward VII on 6 May 1910 plunged London into mourning and theatres closed. Discouraged by failing health and the stresses of theatrical work, James did not renew his efforts in the theatre, but recycled his plays as successful novels. The Outcry was a best-seller in the United States when it was published in 1911. During the years 1890–1893 when he was most engaged with the theatre, James wrote a good deal of theatrical criticism and assisted Elizabeth Robins and others in translating and producing Henrik Ibsen for the first time in London.

Leon Edel argued in his psychoanalytic biography that James was traumatised by the opening night uproar that greeted Guy Domville, and that it plunged him into a prolonged depression. The successful later novels, in Edel's view, were the result of a kind of self-analysis, expressed in fiction, which partly freed him from his fears. Other biographers and scholars have not accepted this account, however; the more common view being that of F.O. Matthiessen, who wrote: "Instead of being crushed by the collapse of his hopes [for the theatre]... he felt a resurgence of new energy."

Non-fiction

Beyond his fiction, James was one of the more important literary critics in the history of the novel. In his classic essay The Art of Fiction (1884), he argued against rigid prescriptions on the novelist's choice of subject and method of treatment. He maintained that the widest possible freedom in content and approach would help ensure narrative fiction's continued vitality.

James wrote many valuable critical articles on other novelists; typical is his book-length study of Nathaniel Hawthorne, which has been the subject of critical debate. Richard Brodhead has suggested that the study was emblematic of James's struggle with Hawthorne's influence, and constituted an effort to place the elder writer "at a disadvantage." Gordon Fraser, meanwhile, has suggested that the study was part of a more commercial effort by James to introduce himself to British readers as Hawthorne's natural successor.

When James assembled the New York Edition of his fiction in his final years, he wrote a series of prefaces that subjected his own work to searching, occasionally harsh criticism.

At 22 James wrote The Noble School of Fiction for The Nation's first issue in 1865. He would write, in all, over 200 essays and book, art, and theatre reviews for the magazine.

For most of his life James harboured ambitions for success as a playwright. He converted his novel The American into a play that enjoyed modest returns in the early 1890s. In all he wrote about a dozen plays, most of which went unproduced. His costume drama Guy Domville failed disastrously on its opening night in 1895. James then largely abandoned his efforts to conquer the stage and returned to his fiction. In his Notebooks he maintained that his theatrical experiment benefited his novels and tales by helping him dramatise his characters' thoughts and emotions. James produced a small but valuable amount of theatrical criticism, including perceptive appreciations of Henrik Ibsen.

With his wide-ranging artistic interests, James occasionally wrote on the visual arts. Perhaps his most valuable contribution was his favourable assessment of fellow expatriate John Singer Sargent, a painter whose critical status has improved markedly in recent decades. James also wrote sometimes charming, sometimes brooding articles about various places he visited and lived in. His most famous books of travel writing include Italian Hours (an example of the charming approach) and The American Scene (most definitely on the brooding side).

James was one of the great letter-writers of any era. More than ten thousand of his personal letters are extant, and over three thousand have been published in a large number of collections. A complete edition of James's letters began publication in 2006, edited by Pierre Walker and Greg Zacharias. As of 2014, eight volumes have been published, covering the period from 1855 to 1880. James's correspondents included celebrated contemporaries like Robert Louis Stevenson, Edith Wharton and Joseph Conrad, along with many others in his wide circle of friends and acquaintances. The letters range from the "mere twaddle of graciousness" to serious discussions of artistic, social and personal issues.

Very late in life James began a series of autobiographical works: A Small Boy and Others, Notes of a Son and Brother, and the unfinished The Middle Years. These books portray the development of a classic observer who was passionately interested in artistic creation but was somewhat reticent about participating fully in the life around him.

Reception

Criticism, biographies and fictional treatments

James's work has remained steadily popular with the limited audience of educated readers to whom he spoke during his lifetime, and has remained firmly in the canon, but, after his death, some American critics, such as Van Wyck Brooks, expressed hostility towards James for his long expatriation and eventual naturalisation as a British subject. Other critics such as E. M. Forster complained about what they saw as James's squeamishness in the treatment of sex and other possibly controversial material, or dismissed his late style as difficult and obscure, relying heavily on extremely long sentences and excessively latinate language. Similarly Oscar Wilde criticised him for writing "fiction as if it were a painful duty". Vernon Parrington, composing a canon of American literature, condemned James for having cut himself off from America. Jorge Luis Borges wrote about him, "Despite the scruples and delicate complexities of James, his work suffers from a major defect: the absence of life." And Virginia Woolf, writing to Lytton Strachey, asked, "Please tell me what you find in Henry James. ... we have his works here, and

I read, and I can't find anything but faintly tinged rose water, urbane and sleek, but vulgar and pale as Walter Lamb. Is there really any sense in it?" The novelist W. Somerset Maugham wrote, "He did not know the English as an Englishman instinctively knows them and so his English characters never to my mind quite ring true," and argued "The great novelists, even in seclusion, have lived life passionately. Henry James was content to observe it from a window." Maugham nevertheless wrote, "The fact remains that those last novels of his, notwithstanding their unreality, make all other novels, except the very best, unreadable." Colm Tóibín observed that James "never really wrote about the English very well. His English characters don't work for me."

Despite these criticisms, James is now valued for his psychological and moral realism, his masterful creation of character, his low-key but playful humour, and his assured command of the language. In his 1983 book, The Novels of Henry James, Edward Wagenknecht offers an assessment that echoes Theodora Bosanquet's:

> "To be completely great," Henry James wrote in an early review, "a work of art must lift up the heart," and his own novels do this to an outstanding degree ... More than sixty years after his death, the great novelist who sometimes professed to have no opinions stands foursquare in the great Christian humanistic and democratic tradition. The men and women who, at the height of World War II, raided the secondhand shops for his out-of-print books knew what they were about. For no writer ever raised a braver banner to which all who love freedom might adhere.

William Dean Howells saw James as a representative of a new realist school of literary art which broke with the English romantic tradition epitomised by the works of Charles Dickens and William Makepeace Thackeray. Howells wrote that realism found "its chief exemplar in Mr. James... A novelist he is not, after the old fashion, or after any fashion but his own." F.R. Leavis championed Henry James as a novelist of "established pre-eminence" in The Great Tradition (1948), asserting that The Portrait of a Lady and The Bostonians were "the two most brilliant novels in the language." James is now prized as a master of point of view who moved literary fiction forward by insisting in showing, not telling, his stories to the reader. (Source: Wikipedia)

NOTABLE WORKS

NOVELS

Watch and Ward (1871)

Roderick Hudson (1875)

The American (1877)

The Europeans (1878)

Confidence (1879)

Washington Square (1880)

The Portrait of a Lady (1881)

The Bostonians (1886)

The Princess Casamassima (1886)

The Reverberator (1888)

The Tragic Muse (1890)

The Other House (1896)

The Spoils of Poynton (1897)

What Maisie Knew (1897)

The Awkward Age (1899)

The Sacred Fount (1901)

The Wings of the Dove (1902)

The Ambassadors (1903)

The Golden Bowl (1904)

The Whole Family (collaborative novel with eleven other authors, 1908

The Outcry (1911)

The Ivory Tower (unfinished, published posthumously 1917)

The Sense of the Past (unfinished, published posthumously 1917)

SHORT STORIES AND NOVELLAS

A Tragedy of Error (1864)

The Story of a Year (1865)

A Landscape Painter (1866)

A Day of Days (1866)

My Friend Bingham (1867)

Poor Richard (1867)

The Story of a Masterpiece (1868)

A Most Extraordinary Case (1868)

A Problem (1868)

De Grey: A Romance (1868)

Osborne's Revenge (1868)

The Romance of Certain Old Clothes (1868)

A Light Man (1869)

Gabrielle de Bergerac (1869)

Travelling Companions (1870)

A Passionate Pilgrim (1871)

At Isella (1871)

Master Eustace (1871)

Guest's Confession (1872)

The Madonna of the Future (1873)

The Sweetheart of M. Briseux (1873)

The Last of the Valerii (1874)

Madame de Mauves (1874)

Adina (1874)

Professor Fargo (1874)

Eugene Pickering (1874)

Benvolio (1875)

Crawford's Consistency (1876)

The Ghostly Rental (1876)

Four Meetings (1877)

Rose-Agathe (1878, as Théodolinde)

Daisy Miller (1878)

Longstaff's Marriage (1878)

An International Episode (1878)

The Pension Beaurepas (1879)

A Diary of a Man of Fifty (1879)

A Bundle of Letters (1879)

The Point of View (1882)

The Siege of London (1883)

Impressions of a Cousin (1883)

Lady Barberina (1884)

Pandora (1884)

The Author of Beltraffio (1884)

Georgina's Reasons (1884)

A New England Winter (1884)

The Path of Duty (1884)

Mrs. Temperly (1887)

Louisa Pallant (1888)

The Aspern Papers (1888)

The Liar (1888)

The Modern Warning (1888, originally published as The Two Countries)

A London Life (1888)

The Patagonia (1888)

The Lesson of the Master (1888)

The Solution (1888)

The Pupil (1891)

Brooksmith (1891)

The Marriages (1891)

The Chaperon (1891)

Sir Edmund Orme (1891)

Nona Vincent (1892)

The Real Thing (1892)

The Private Life (1892)

Lord Beaupré (1892)

The Visits (1892)

Sir Dominick Ferrand (1892)

Greville Fane (1892)

Collaboration (1892)

Owen Wingrave (1892)

The Wheel of Time (1892)

The Middle Years (1893)

The Death of the Lion (1894)

The Coxon Fund (1894)

The Next Time (1895)

Glasses (1896)

The Altar of the Dead (1895)

The Figure in the Carpet (1896)

The Way It Came (1896, also published as The Friends of the Friends)

The Turn of the Screw (1898)

Covering End (1898)

In the Cage (1898)

John Delavoy (1898)

The Given Case (1898)

Europe (1899)

The Great Condition (1899)

The Real Right Thing (1899)

Paste (1899)

The Great Good Place (1900)

Maud-Evelyn (1900)

Miss Gunton of Poughkeepsie (1900)

The Tree of Knowledge (1900)

The Abasement of the Northmores (1900)

The Third Person (1900)

The Special Type (1900)

The Tone of Time (1900)

Broken Wings (1900)

The Two Faces (1900)

Mrs. Medwin (1901)

The Beldonald Holbein (1901)

The Story in It (1902)

Flickerbridge (1902)

The Birthplace (1903)

The Beast in the Jungle (1903)

The Papers (1903)

Fordham Castle (1904)

Julia Bride (1908)

The Jolly Corner (1908)

The Velvet Glove (1909)

Mora Montravers (1909)

Crapy Cornelia (1909)

The Bench of Desolation (1909)

A Round of Visits (1910)

OTHER

Transatlantic Sketches (1875)

French Poets and Novelists (1878)

Hawthorne (1879)

Portraits of Places (1883)

A Little Tour in France (1884)

Partial Portraits (1888)

Essays in London and Elsewhere (1893)

Picture and Text (1893)

Terminations (1893)

Theatricals (1894)

Theatricals: Second Series (1895)

Guy Domville (1895)

The Soft Side (1900)

William Wetmore Story and His Friends (1903)

The Better Sort (1903)

English Hours (1905)

The Question of our Speech; The Lesson of Balzac. Two Lectures (1905)

The American Scene (1907)

Views and Reviews (1908)

Italian Hours (1909)

A Small Boy and Others (1913)

Notes on Novelists (1914)

Notes of a Son and Brother (1914)

Within the Rim (1918)

Travelling Companions (1919)

Notebooks (various, published posthumously)

The Middle Years (unfinished, published posthumously 1917)

A Most Unholy Trade (1925, published posthumously)

The Art of the Novel : Critical Prefaces (1934)

CPSIA information can be obtained
at www.ICGtesting.com
Printed in the USA
LVHW091914261020
669864LV00002B/14